THE DEFIANCE

A SHAWNEE ADVENTURE

THE DEFIANCE

A SHAWNEE ADVENTURE

BOB GIEL

HAT CREEK

HAT CREEK

an imprint of
Roan & Weatherford Publishing Associates, LLC
Bentonville, Arkansas • Heber City, Utah
www.roanweatherford.com

Library of Congress Cataloging-in-Publication Data
Names: Giel, Bob, author
Title: The Defiance/Bob Giel | Shawnee #5
Description: First Edition. | Bentonville: Hat Creek, 2026.
Identifiers: | 979-8-89299-126-1 (trade paperback) | ISBN: 979-8-89299-127-8 (eBook)
Subjects: FICTION/Westerns | FICTION/Action & Adventure |
FICTION/Mystery & Detective/General

Hat Creek trade paperback edition April, 2026

Cover & Interior Design by Casey W. Cowan
Cover art by Frederic Remington (1861-1909)
Aiding a Comrade, Oil on canvas, 1890
Editing by Lisa Lindsey & Amy Cowan

For Sandy Bostwick

1

IVILIZATION, FINALLY... OR THE CLOSEST thing to it, at least! It wasn't much, at least the picture painted in waves of rising heat in the distance gave that impression. Maybe just a settlement, but it would have to do. Hungry, tired and broke, Victor Garand had little choice. Stumbling, unsure of his steps, he moved toward it.

He'd been on the trail for the better part of a week, making his way west from a washed-up gold camp called Yreka where he had hoped to find his fortune. Instead, he found desolation, played out mines and panned out streams, and a population consisting mostly of ne'er-do-wells and downright criminals whose only intention was to bilk ordinary citizens of their possessions. He'd been a victim of that, not that he'd had much to lose, but amounts hadn't mattered, only the fact he'd had something they didn't, and now they did. Leaving Yreka in the middle of the night, fearing for his life, with only a few coins left in his pocket, he'd struck out on foot in search of better digs.

Moving west made sense. He'd heard talk in Yreka of new gold fields turning up in that direction, but it was just general conversation, nothing specific. So, he moved aimlessly, with no food or water, save for what he could scrounge off the land, and no weapons, baking in the hot California summer sun. This day would be no better, and it was not even noon yet. This was crazy. There had to be a better way.

If there was one, he was not aware of it and was too worn out to try to conceive of one. One thing was sure. He should never have left Illinois in the first place.

Garand moved slowly, unsteadily, trying to stay in the shade of a tree line or in the shadows of boulders. He glanced again at the image in the distance. It definitely resembled a cluster of buildings. As he drew closer, he could make out the outlines of structures, strung together in an orderly fashion. That would be a bit of a rarity in these parts. Most of the settlements he'd seen were just a bunch of tents and huts thrown together haphazardly. He'd keep going toward it in the hope of finding at least a few welcoming faces, perhaps work of some sort that would allow him to become human again. It was too soon to look beyond that.

He thanked God for small things, like the slouch hat on his head, whose wide brim offered some protection from the sun. And he was glad that the once-white collarless dress shirt he'd worn as part of the suit he no longer owned had long sleeves to keep the skin on his arms from burning. He was a mess, but his appearance was the least of his worries. His main concern was survival. To accomplish that, he had to make it to that town up ahead.

He could only stagger as he progressed toward that image in the distance. Was it real or merely a mirage? At this point, who knew?

Exhausted, on the verge of passing out, Garand's head pounded. Sight became blurred. The sign on the side of what was hardly a road supported him as he clung to it to keep from falling. Maybe he'd lost consciousness for a moment because he couldn't recall the steps that brought him to the signpost.

He took a minute to collect himself, took a deep breath, and shook the cobwebs from his head. That didn't work except to sharpen his vision some, but he couldn't stay here in this position indefinitely, not when survival was just a few steps away. He pushed back to see and study the sign. *Colinas de Oro,* it read. Curious. Spanish, probably, a language he did not understand. He went on, stumbling toward the buildings that were blurred in his vision, but seemed tangible, within reach.

The widening of the road that became the single dirt street of this town gave a silent welcome to the staggering, almost out of it, stranger. An errant concern for his appearance came and went in less than a second. His gaze settled on the water trough on one side, and he made for it. He could see the water surface in there, still, not even rippling because there was no breeze. Another fleeting concern, that it was probably not clean, got tossed aside as his last step became a stumble that put him on his knees at the side of the trough. He grasped the wood to stop his fall and then pulled himself toward the fluid, dropping his hat beside him. He cupped his hands and dipped out a helping. Yes, it was hot, yes, it was foul-tasting, but it was water. It would do the job of hydrating him, and that was all that concerned him. If it served its purpose and later came back up, so be it. He would drink his fill.

As the water went down, tasting a bit foul, probably from sitting in the trough in the sun for longer than it should, Garand became vaguely aware of something, or someone, watching him. It wasn't very apparent, maybe he was imagining it, but it seemed he wasn't alone on the deserted street. He looked up abruptly, water dripping from his mouth and hands, his eyes darting here and there. He saw nothing. Shaking his head at his overactive imagination, he went back for more water.

When his thirst was quenched, Garand splashed water in his face and over his head. He made a contented grunt. Slapping his hat on his soaking head, he hauled himself up on unsteady legs and glanced around, this time to observe his surroundings. He moved slowly toward the end of the trough, concentrating on walking. Water from his hair coursed down his face and dripped onto his grimy shirt.

His eyes took in several of the businesses lining the street across from him. One attracted him more than the others—the saloon, marked *Taylor's* in black paint on the facade above the batwing doors, and the sign in the window advertising a free lunch tugged at him as hunger replaced thirst as his primary requirement.

Crossing the street in a wobbly, almost drunken walk, he still had the vague impression he was being watched. But hunger had replaced any desire to resolve the thought.

He stepped through the swinging doors into an interior smaller than the exterior made it appear. Situated in the rear of the room, the plain wooden bar took up the entire width. Behind it, a squat, balding man in a soiled white shirt stood with his hands leaning against it. To the sides, roughhewn tables and chairs were randomly placed. At one end of the bar, a tray of sliced meats and cheeses sat open with stacks of sliced bread around it. Flies were already grouped around the tray in abundance. Garand focused on the food and veered toward it. As he grabbed two slices of bread and reached for the meat, a gruff voice stopped him.

"That ain't free without you buy a drink."

Garand stopped dead and looked around for the source. The short man behind the bar moved quickly to where he stood. "What'll you have?"

Without replying, Garand dug into his pants pocket for the few coins in his possession. He placed them on the bar. "Will this buy me a beer?"

"Nah! That ain't enough."

Crushed, Garand stared at the man, his mouth open, with the blank expression of one at his wits end.

"May I be of assistance?" The words were distant, almost not even there. Then the graveled, age-tinged voice came through more clearly as did the Germanic accent.

Garand looked around at a slight man with a full gray beard and dilapidated clothes gazing at him from a few feet away. He was supported by a crutch that ran from his underarm down his right side. His head was cocked to one side. He had an inquisitive expression on his wrinkled face, that portion of it not hidden by the beard. He stared down at Garand, but he said nothing further.

Confused, exhausted, unsure of this stranger and his own circumstances, Garand mumbled something about not having enough money.

"Allow me." The man's voice was stronger now, or at least it seemed so to Garand. He dropped a coin on the bar next to Garand's offering. "That should suffice."

The bartender scooped up the money and turned away to fill the order. Mumbling a thank you to his benefactor, Garand returned to his assault on the food tray. As he assembled his sandwich and took the vigorous initial bite, a beer mug was placed in front of him. Over his shoulder, he heard the old man's voice.

"Was that your only money?"

His mouth too full of food to speak, he nodded instead. Savoring the taste, he swallowed hard and chased it with the room-temperature brew.

"That is unfortunate." The old man actually looked contrite.

Garand cleared his throat. "That's all right. I'm used to it by now." He took another bite.

"My name is Zoltan Hirsch."

Now returning to a somewhat human state, Garand reacted favorably to the man's attempt at civility, extending his hand. "Victor Garand." They shook hands.

Hirsch smiled. "We can sit." He gestured to an unoccupied table nearby. "It's all right. I have means."

Garand picked up his half empty glass and followed Hirsch to the table. Hirsch turned toward the bar and raised his voice. "May we have two glasses of beer here, please?" The bartender nodded. Hirsch sat across from Garand and placed the crutch between his legs, the top with the shoulder brace resting on his chest. Garand finished his food.

"Get more if you like." Hirsch pointed to the lunch tray.

Garand liked that idea and went back for another sandwich. When he returned, the two beer mugs had been placed by the bartender, who stood by.

"I will settle the bill when I leave." Hirsch flashed a mild smile at the man. The statement was acknowledged with a nod. The barkeep left them.

Garand sat again. Hirsch seemed to anticipate his question about the money, but Garand was still too preoccupied with eating to be immediately concerned. He would delay that in favor of filling his belly.

Another sandwich and two beers later, Garand wiped a dirty sleeve across his mouth. "Thank you for the drinks. Unfortunately, I have no way of repaying you."

Hirsch waved a hand. "Think no more of it."

"I am curious, though. Our meeting… I get the feeling it was not a coincidence."

Hirsch leaned in. "You are correct. I watched you stumble into the town, and I decided to make your acquaintance."

Garand's blank stare had to have been apparent. "May I ask why?"

Hirsch smiled. "I thought you might be a good prospect."

Now confused, Garand allowed the curiosity to flow. "Prospect? For what?"

"I might have an attractive offer to make you."

Garand's eyes glazed over. Who was this person? What did he want? "What offer?"

Hirsch raised a halting hand. "I need to learn more about you first. Do you mind answering a few questions?"

Garand thought for a second. "You've staked me food and drink without requiring repayment. I'm grateful for that, so I suppose a few answers couldn't hurt anything."

Hirsch's smile broadened. "Tell me about Victor Garand. What brought you to this forsaken place and your current circumstances?"

Garand took a breath. "I come from Illinois where I was a teacher. My position was nothing more than sustenance and I had no other prospects, so I decided to come west. I thought, having heard so many stories of people striking it rich in the gold fields, that I might do the same. Needless to say, that did not happen. In the last town I was in, I was put upon by thieves who took everything I owned. I was lucky to escape with my life. I thought, if I go farther west, my luck would improve. So far, the opposite has been true."

Hirsch nodded. "I'm sorry about your circumstances. You're obviously an intelligent man. To leave your life and seek your fortune takes quite some courage. Are you interested in hearing my proposition?"

"If it's a job you're offering, I'll do anything within reason to improve my lot."

"What about something outside the realm of reason?"

Garand squinted at the man. "I don't understand. Are you proposing something illegal. I'm not interested in breaking the law."

Hirsch sat back. "Please allow me to explain." He lowered his voice to barely above a whisper. "I have located a vein of gold in the foothills west of here. I have built the beginnings of a mineshaft and constructed some equipment that is capable of extracting and refining the ore." He reached inside his shirt and pulled a sack halfway out to illustrate. "This is the product of my labors. There is much more out there to be had. When I was processing this, I had an accident that weakened my leg enough to prevent me from doing the heavy work necessary. The leg has lost most of its strength, and I am dependent on this piece of wood"—he indicated the crutch—"to get around. Because of this, I am forced to seek out a partner, a person who can do what I cannot, for an equal share of the proceeds."

Garand showed interest. "You're referring to me?"

Hirsch replaced the sack. "Yes."

"But you don't know anything about me."

"You've told me all I need to know. You are physically capable of doing the work. One look at you answers that question." Hirsch shook his head. "You are intelligent, and you do not strike me as the violent type. I am willing to take the chance. Are you?"

Garand, taken aback by the proposal, hesitated as he tried to get this straight in his mind. However, that mind was now beginning to cloud over, affected by a combination of exhaustion and now alcohol. He started questioning the sincerity of the man across from him. Was this a joke, an elaborate hoax? "I… I don't know. What specifically are you asking me to do?" Though he was certain he knew what Hirsch's answer would be, he needed to hear it in detail.

"To become my partner, my equal partner in the mine. The reality is that I cannot work the mine in my condition, and, at this point, I do not have the money to pay someone to work it. Since half is better than nothing at all, I am willing to share the proceeds equally with a partner who is capable of doing the physical labor required, which I cannot do. It could be you."

Garand shook his head, both to clear it and to indicate his amazement. "But I'm a stranger. Why not choose someone you're acquainted with, someone here in this town?"

Hirsch's expression became dire. "There is not one soul in this town I would choose. I have seen things and heard things about most of them that tells me none are trustworthy. They would jump my claim at the first chance opportunity."

Garand leaned in. "How do you know *I* won't jump your claim or murder you in your sleep?"

Hirsch leaned forward. "Of course I do not. But I am a fairly good judge of character. The fact that you are questioning me instead of simply accepting my offer, and your aversion to anything illegal, tells me you have moral standards, ethics. I am willing to take the chance that I am right."

Garand took a deep breath. "This is crazy. I've never heard anything like this before."

"You have never been presented with a situation like this before." Hirsch looked around as if being watched. "Think of it, Garand. I am offering you half interest in a lucrative endeavor and all I require in return is your brawn to be combined with my brains. I am an engineer. I know how these things need to be done. There are still tasks I *can* do, like building and cooking while you work. Join me, and you will see that this is the chance of a lifetime. It demands no investment on your part, except for your sweat effort. It can make you a rich man. I swear to you, it is there for the taking."

Garand found himself drawn in. This, after all, was the reason he'd come west, to make his fortune. Was it so farfetched that it could fall into his lap, with physical work the only requirement? No doubt, stranger things have happened. Hirsch was right about one thing, Garand's situation made him an ideal candidate. Despite this going against his analytical nature, every fiber in his being cried out for change. It was time. Truthfully, it was far past time. But he still had questions. "Have you registered your claim?"

Hirsch leaned in again. "No. I was about to when my accident convinced me I could not do this alone. I decided then to seek out a partner first. When you are convinced that what I say is true, we will register it together, in both our names."

Garand took another deep breath and looked away in thought. One thing was certain. He'd probably never trip over another opportunity like this in his lifetime. And, all things considered, what did he actually have to lose, a little sweat? "All right, Hirsch, count me in."

Hirsch's face lit up. "Excellent!" He reached across the table and shook hands with Garand. "Excellent."

Garand became totally engrossed. "So, what happens now?"

Hirsch leaned back. "Well, you should be rested when we go to the mine. It is not an easy trip on foot. I only have one mule, and I must ride in my condition, so you will have to walk. I assume you do not have a place to sleep. May I suggest the stable at the west end of the town? My mule is quartered there. Straw in abundance can be fairly comfortable."

Garand smiled. "Lately I've slept on worse."

Hirsch nodded. "I would imagine. In the meantime, we can simply sit here and finish our beer. The food here is acceptable, so we can dine here and then go to the stable. In the morning, we can leave for the mine."

"It would seem you have it all figured out."

Hirsch smiled and nodded. "Yes, that is what I do."

IN THE COOL MORNING, THEY traveled the seven mile stretch of beaten down earth that was the west road out of Colinas de Oro. Hirsch rode his supply laden mule. Garand trudged along on foot beside them. Both were silent. Garand was certainly curious to see this mining operation Hirsch had spoken of, but he did not voice the many questions he had. He would see the answers soon enough and would probably have many more queries at that time. That would be soon enough to make himself annoying.

As well, he wondered about Hirsch himself, had concerns about the man's mental stability. It wasn't anything concrete, but funny ways the man had and strange statements he'd made had fostered those thoughts. He'd seemed very guarded about the mine, to the point of distraction. He trusted no one, one of the reasons he had not yet registered his claim. His intention seemed to be to keep its existence secret until he was able to prove conclusively that it was lucrative. Then, and only then, would he register it in a public ceremony of sorts that would establish his unquestioned ownership, thereby preventing an attempt at claim jumping. "One cannot be too careful," he'd said on more than one occasion throughout their evening conversations.

Because of that, Garand questioned why Hirsch seemed to place so much trust in his new companion—partner. Why had he even chosen Garand to begin with? This was a unique situation, driven by a unique individual, to say the least, but Garand was far enough into it now that he would see it through and ask questions when necessary. What other choice did he have, save for continuing life as a destitute roustabout?

After a while, the main road continued straight ahead toward a stand of trees while an obscure, tree-lined trail jutted off to the right. A cluster of large boulders could be seen in the distance beyond the trail. Garand took these to be the foothills Hirsch had mentioned the day before. Hirsch led the way onto the trail. Garand stayed with him, walking beside the mule.

"The mine is a short distance along this path. The path ends at the base of the mountain." They went on silently for about a mile.

As they approached the dead end, rocks gradually replaced the trees. The trail widened into a small box canyon, the location of the mine, surrounded by steep hillsides to the left and right, and an almost perpendicular rock wall in the rear that rose to tower over the canyon. Hirsch stopped when they entered the area.

Garand looked around carefully, surprised at the level of development already in place. In the far right corner, near where the north side slope met the back wall, a rudimentary cabin had been built. A mine shaft, shored with wood cut from nearby trees, had been opened in the mountain surface on the left hand side of the back wall. From the weathered look of the visible shoring timbers, the shaft appeared to have been there for quite some time. More than likely, the existence of the hut was of similar age. Garand wondered if the structures predated Hirsch's finding of the mine. He deferred the question.

Closer in the foreground along the left wall stood several pieces of equipment. Based on his limited knowledge of mining, gleaned from previous experience at other operations he'd worked during his trek west, Garand guessed at their uses—a stamping apparatus used to crush the rocks extracted from the mine which were believed to contain gold ore, a rocker box used to wash away loose dirt, and a makeshift smelting table to liberate the gold from its stone encasements.

Hirsch slid off the mule and leaned against it for support. "Well, Garand, here it is. I call it "The Defiance" because it defies convention. You will see. It will make us both rich men."

2

OR THE FIRST TIME IN fifteen years, Alonzo Pearce took a hotel room and signed in using his own name without the concern of being arrested. He walked unguarded to his room and dropped his gear. When he heard a knock on the door, he opened it to find Rhiann Swayze, tall and well proportioned, in a flattering burgundy dress. He smiled.

She remained in the doorway. "I saw you come into the lobby. Governor Wallace asked to see you as soon as you arrived. I'm sure it has to do with your amnesty."

"Well, I ain't all that presentable, but I can go now, if'n that's all right."

"You look fine to me. Would you like some company?"

His smile broadened. "Surely would. You being part and parcel of this, you should ought to be there."

She placed her hand in the crook of his arm. "Shall we?"

"Yes, ma'am, we shall."

THEY WALKED ARM IN ARM from the hotel to the Palace of the Governors, the center of government in Santa Fe, New Mexico Territory. Steeped in the tradition of the Spanish possession it once was, the palace reflected the influence of its forebears in its adobe walls and fifteenth century architecture.

As they moved along, Rhiann's memory drifted back to her first meeting with Alonzo Pearce in her capacity as a Pinkerton agent, it had taken her months to complete her assignment. She was to locate him and offer him a chance for amnesty. Fifteen years earlier, circumstances had forced him into the life of a wanted outlaw. Starting there, she tracked him through his outlaw years, learning from witnesses that, under the assumed name of Shawnee, his home town in Kansas, he'd helped many people. Her investigation led her to a mountain top in Mexico where he'd fled to avoid capture. Relating the offer, made by the current governor of New Mexico, Lew Wallace, she convinced him to return to the states to mount an offensive against the band of raiders who threatened the very existence of the territory. In return, were he successful, the governor offered amnesty, a clean slate and a chance to start a new life on the right side of the law. With Rhiann's help, Alonzo, whom she now called Lon, broke up the ring and returned law and order to New Mexico.

Entering the palace, they went straight to the governor's office. As they stepped inside, the governor's secretary, a pleasant-looking young woman with spectacles and mousey brown hair pulled back in a bun, greeted them.

"Good day, may I help you?"

"Good day," Rhiann spoke up. "Alonzo Pearce and Rhiann Swayze to see the governor."

"Oh, yes, Governor Wallace is expecting you." The woman got up and tapped on the door to the inner office. Opening the door, she peeked in. "Mister Pearce and Miss Swayze, sir."

"Yes, send them in."

The woman opened the door fully and stood aside. Lon and Rhiann stepped in.

Governor Wallace, once a general in the Union army during the War Between the States, rose as they entered. He extended his hand to Lon. "Mister Pearce, I can't tell you how grateful I am."

Lon just grinned as he shook hands with the governor.

Wallace turned his attention to Rhiann. "And you, Miss Swayze, you are a constant source of amazement to me. You've gone well above and beyond the call of any duty you've taken on. I intend to commend you highly to Mister Pinkerton. Thank you."

Rhiann smiled. "You're very kind, sir."

"Please, sit down." Wallace sat as they took seats in front of him. "You might be interested in the developments of this past week. Our investigation of Yaeger and Hardrick has turned up the names of quite a few members of this government who were involved in some way in Yaeger's scheme. As an aside, we determined that Hardrick's sick mother, whom he constantly used as an excuse for his absences, is nonexistent. She died several years ago. Several of the suspects have already been identified as being involved in the Santa Fe Ring. Indictments will be forthcoming."

Wallace's smile changed to a frown.

"Unfortunately, the ring itself is still basically intact and is powerful enough to resist any efforts I can put forth to disrupt them. Now they've gone completely underground." The governor breathed a sigh and looked off into space. "Quite frankly, I'm at my wits end, and I'm exhausted. I've asked the president to send a replacement for this office. Someone else can continue this fight. I plan to retire and pursue my writing. However, right now, to the business at hand."

He pushed back from his desk and reached into the top drawer. Bringing out a sheet of paper, he signed it at the bottom, blotted the signature, and handed the document to Lon. "This is your proclamation of amnesty. It is legal and within the bounds of my authority as a federal officer, therefore, it applies throughout the United States. Before I leave office, I will endeavor to have destroyed as many wanted posters with your name on them as we can find. However, I can only order that within this territory. If you leave New Mexico, keep that document handy. It will save you some difficulty if a wanted poster turns up."

Lon took the paper and looked it over. Wallace handed him an envelope bearing the imprint of the territorial government. Lon folded the page and placed it in the envelope.

Wallace's smile returned. "Now you are a free man as long as you do not break any additional laws. As I told you once before, if you do, as Billy Bonney did, you will answer for that offense. Do you understand the terms?"

"Reckon so. I screw up and I'm right back where I started."

"Essentially, yes."

"I give you my word, Governor, I ain't going to screw this up."

"I'm sure you won't."

They rose in unison. Wallace shook Lon's hand once more.

"Again, more thanks than I can say."

"None needed, Governor. You said it all here." Lon pointed at the amnesty paper.

Wallace turned to Rhiann. "It's been a distinct pleasure knowing you, Miss Swayze."

"For me as well, sir."

Lon and Rhiann went to the door.

Wallace called out after them. "God speed to you both."

They both said their thanks and left. As they exited the building, Rhiann stopped and turned to Lon.

"So, do you have any plans for the future, now that you have one?"

Lon's hand went to the back of his neck. "Well, first off, keep my nose clean, stay out of trouble. Head west, I reckon. Somewheres I ain't knowed. California, maybe. Maybe up north. Get a job. Save up some money. Start up a little spread. Run some cattle. Learned all about that working the Tell Ranch. Reckon that'll do for starters."

She laid her hand on his arm and smiled. There was more on her mind, and she struggled to put it into words. "Sounds like you've been thinking about that for quite a while. Have you… considered taking… someone along with you, someone… to keep you company?"

Lon smiled at her. "Like you, maybe?"

Rhiann smiled back. "Uh-huh." She saw the blood rush into his face in an uninhibited blush.

"Well, now." His hand stayed at the back of his neck. "That surely sounds like something I'd admire to do."

Her smile broadened into a genuine grin. Her hand tightened on his arm. "Wonderful."

They walked away from the building into the more typical surroundings of wood and adobe structures present in most frontier towns and cities. In unison, their steps sounded on the boardwalk leading back to the hotel.

Rhiann fell silent. Her mind was still not clear. She had more to say, but she'd reached the point where decorum told her it was not her place to continue. However, considering what they'd just been through, the risk to both their lives, convention be damned. She had something to say, and she was damn well going to say it. "Lon."

But, as she spoke, he said her name in the same breath. She stopped, and they both chuckled at the juxtaposition of thoughts. A brief, awkward silence followed.

She took the initiative. "Go ahead."

"I been pondering something else, another part of the future, and I got to ask you…." He trailed off, stopping in mid step. A struggling expression replaced his smile.

She turned to him. "Ask me what?"

He hesitated, sloughing his foot nervously, pursing his lips.

"Lon?"

"Aw, I ain't much good at this, ain't sure how it's supposed to go."

Rhiann sought to settle his uneasiness. "Lon, it's all right. You can ask me anything."

He removed his hat and steeled himself, speaking slowly, thoughtfully. "I ain't got the right words and all, but here goes. Rhiann Swayze, I got real deep feelings for you, and I'd surely be pleased and proud if you'd consent to marry."

Unconsciously, Rhiann's mouth fell open as his words sank in. She was silent for a long time. In truth, she was not surprised. There had been signs of his feelings throughout their journey from Mexico, during their collaboration in taking down the Yaeger organization. His comfort in the aftermath of her killing Yaeger to save Lon's life got her through a bad time. His effort to save her from drowning in the Rio Grande not only demonstrated his feelings for her, but convinced her she loved him. Her every action thereafter led to this point.

He turned away. "It's all right, you don't have to say nothing. I should a knowed it was too much to put on you."

Instinctively, she tugged on his sleeve, pulling him to face her. She smiled warmly but decided on actions in place of words. She reached behind his neck, pulled his head down the inch or so it took to make their heights equal, and kissed him, softly at first, then with more intensity. He kissed her back, readily.

Their arms wrapped around each other in a close embrace, holding each other tightly. When the kiss ended seconds later, Rhiann leaned her head back.

He gazed at her hesitantly. "I'm ciphering that to be a yes."

She grinned, finding herself remarkably composed in a trying circumstance. "I'm not in the habit of saying no with a kiss." She nodded, almost involuntarily. "So, yes, my answer is yes."

He matched her grin. "Whooee! That's a relief! If you knowed how long I been kicking that around in my head—"

"Probably as long as I have."

They stood for a second, staring at each other. Then he kissed her again. "I kinda like doing that."

"Yeah, me too."

"Reckon we should ought a do something about this."

Feeling playful, she feigned a concerned expression. "Any thoughts?"

"Well, kinda sorta. Truth be told, I been pondering on that as well. It's a kinda long, hard way to go, but I's considering if'n *Padre* Cortez was to say them words to make it legal and binding, that'd surely mean a lot to me."

Rhiann smiled again, remembering the priest who helped her find Lon in Mexico. "Back to Mexico? I'm not a Catholic, you know."

"I ain't even close to one neither. You know, a good friend once told me he didn't care I's purple and I worshipped a prairie dog. How you believe don't make no neverminds to me, and from what I know about the *padre*, it won't make no neverminds to him neither."

Her smile broadened. "Nor to me. *Padre* Cortez it will be."

Lon looked around as if something hovered over them. "Whooee! This is like a dream come true. Say, I surely want to kiss on you some more."

She held him close. "As much as you want."

"I want you to know I won't go no further till the *padre* says them words on us."

She leaned in to kiss him. "I know you won't, and I love you for it."

They kissed again, and Lon looked around, again blushing.

"You reckon maybe we should ought to go find someplace private-like? We putting on a kind of a show here."

Rhiann looked over her shoulder at the prying eyes of locals, stopping to observe their actions. "I don't much care, but, yeah, you might be right."

Lon wrapped a protective arm around her waist. They moved along.

THE NEXT DAY, RHIANN, IN a less formal print dress, left the hotel with Lon beside her. "I have to send the telegram to Mister Pinkerton. To save time, why don't you start getting the supplies together? I'll meet you at the mercantile before you're finished."

Lon nodded and stepped off the hotel porch, crossing the street to the general store.

Rhiann entered the telegraph office and picked up the pad and pencil provided at the operator's cage against the back wall. She listed the recipient as Allan Pinkerton, Pinkerton Detective Agency, Chicago, poised the pencil at the next line, and then stopped. She knew exactly what must be said, but finding the words to fit in a wire would take some thought and effort.

She'd been a Pinkerton investigator for close to five years, one of the organization's first female operatives and likely the youngest, still in her twenties. To hear Pinkerton tell it, one of the best. Having learned her trade well and having excelled in the position, Rhiann had become one of Pinkerton's most trusted employees. To now turn around, without warning, and tender her resignation would take proper wording so as not to come off as ungrateful for the opportunity. She owed Mr. Pinkerton at least that much for having taken a chance in hiring the green, young daughter of a Minneapolis police officer who'd been informally schooled in her father's profession and had paid close attention to every lesson. "Don't burn your bridges," her father had told her more than once.

She'd listened.

As Rhiann stared at the nearly blank page, she concluded that this brief space available was not the vehicle to convey what must be expressed. That would take a hand written letter and much more extensive thought to be executed in the days to come. She wrote,

Resigning position effective immediately to marry. Please wire all back pay and expenses c/o Western Union Santa Fe. Letter of explanation to follow. Rhiann Swayze

Putting down the pencil, she tore off the sheet and handed it and the prescribed fee inside the cage to the balding telegrapher. He read the message and smiled up at her. She flashed a smile in response and left the place as the telegraph key began clicking.

A short walk brought Rhiann to the mercantile storefront where she found Lon involved in compiling the items for the supply outfit their Mexico trip would require. She entered as the clerk finished boxing the items.

Lon turned as she reached him. "Just about got what we need here."

The clerk handed him the bill. "That will be ten dollars and twenty-two cents, sir."

Rhiann stepped up to the counter and opened her purse. She handed the clerk a few coins, and he turned away to make change. At the same time, a surly man in dirty clothes, resembling those of a blacksmith, slid in beside Lon. A strong body odor wafted around him.

"You just a downright moocher, ain't you, boy?" His voice was as grungy as his appearance.

Lon appeared surprised at the incursion. "How's that, friend?"

"Real man don't allow no woman to pay his debts for him. Real man coughs it up on his lonesome."

Lon hesitated a second. "Off hand, I'd say that ain't none of your business. Reckon you oughta back off."

Rhiann recognized Lon's statement as a gentle reminder of the intruder's place. The man took the opposite path.

"You calling me out, fellow?"

"I'm telling you back off. This don't have to go no worse."

The man grumbled. "Hah! So you a yellow-belly as well as a beggar."

Lon turned to face him, lowering his voice ominously. "Don't call me that."

"I'll call you anything I wants. What you going to do about it?"

Rhiann saw it coming. She thought fast to head this off before it got out of hand.

At the same moment, Lon took a handful of the man's Henley shirt, pulling him close, almost nose to nose.

"Lon."

Rhiann's voice stopped further action, but Lon hung on to the shirt and the closeness that went with it. As Lon glared at the intruder and he glared back, Rhiann slipped around behind him, her hand in her purse. She held her breath at the offensive odor he gave off, but she moved in tight all the same. A quick move followed. Her voice was almost at a whisper.

"Sir, the poke you feel in your back is a Colt Lightening revolver. It's loaded, and I know how to use it. Perhaps knowledge of those facts might cause you to rethink your position here."

Lon froze in place as the interloper's expression changed from arrogance to concern. Still, he did not back down. Rhiann pushed the muzzle harder into his flesh.

"Well?" Lon's single word caused movement.

Slowly, the man raised his hands, palms forward. A sheepish grin crossed his face as he attempted to back away, stopped by Rhiann's, and the gun's, presence. "Yeah, sorry, no offense."

Lon released the shirt, staring at the man for a second. "Don't you got someplace you need to be right about now?"

The man side-stepped and backed off a few paces. "Yeah, yeah, sorry." He turned sharply and walked out of the store.

Lon turned slowly to face Rhiann. He was not happy. "Rhiann, what you just done there—"

"Lon, I'm sorry, but you have to understand something." She slipped the gun into her purse and lowered her voice to again. "Everything's changed now. You have to be very careful. You can't go around getting into fights. One arrest and your amnesty goes away. You risked too much to just throw it away over some bully trying to get a rise out of you."

Lon scrunched up his face. "Aw, you're right, I know it. It's just hard to swallow is all. You paying my bills is hard enough, but getting called out on it, well, that was the last straw."

"Lon, I'm not paying your bills. I'm contributing to our bills. We're going to be man and wife. It's not your money or my money anymore—it's our money. If I happen to have more to put in right now than you do, that's just how it is. Your turn will come."

Lon shook his head, pondering. "Reckon there's more to this being married stuff than I ciphered."

"We both have a lot to learn."

"Surely 'pears like you done a lot more cogitating on the how a this than me."

Rhiann smiled. "I guess I've been at it longer. The truth of it is, it's been in the back of my mind since we first met. The longer I've known you and the more we've been through, the more I was convinced we had to be together."

3

A T MIDDAY, VICTOR GARAND STOOD soaked in perspiration at the end of the twelve foot section of shaft already dug out and shored. Hirsch was propped beside him on his crutch, facing the work surface. Behind them, Hirsch's mule stood hitched to a makeshift cart with fixed sides, a removable tailgate, and wooden wheels. The cart was about half full with the product of the current excavation. Garand rested on the handle of a pickaxe propped on its head in front of him. He sucked in gulps of dusty air.

"The vein disappeared here." Hirsch pointed to a spot on the right wall of the shaft. "I believe it runs on a forty-five degree angle further in from this point. You must start a secondary tunnel here."

Garand cleared his throat of the grit accompanying his breaths. "Come on, Hirsch, how can you be so sure of the angle?"

"I know how these things go. I have been doing this in one mine or another for as long as I can remember. You must dig here." He used his hand to illustrate the route. "On this angle."

Garand shook his head. "All right, but I'm going to need more water and more light."

"Yah, I will get those for you. I will also empty the cart." Hirsch turned and went to the mule to lead the animal out of the shaft.

Garand, already tired from this half day of backbreaking work, and now unconvinced of Hirsch's expertise, lifted the pick to begin the new shaft.

With Garand doing most of the physical labor and Hirsch helping where he could, over the next two weeks, they worked their way six feet into the new tunnel, shoring as they went. No traces of gold were found during that time. Frustration consumed Garand who saw no future in further excavation.

They sat in the small log cabin over a meager dinner one night. Garand, lacking an appetite, played with his food. He'd been silent to this point. Finally, he voiced his feelings.

"This is ridiculous. And it's futile. We've been at this for a month now. Whatever gold was in that mine, you've already gotten out. We're beating a dead horse here, and I'm done with it. I'm pulling out in the morning."

Hirsch was appalled. "Garand, you can't be serious. There is gold in there. I know it. I can feel it. We just need a little more time, a little more effort."

Garand dropped his fork loudly and got up. "A little more time, a little more effort? No. All that will give us is what we have now, nothing but the gold in your poke." He turned away.

"No. You must reconsider. We are so close."

Garand turned to face Hirsch. "Close? We're no closer than the day I walked in here. Have you seen even a trace of gold in what I've dug out of that shaft?" He waited for the answer that did not come. "Of course you haven't because there's nothing there." He swiped his hand at Hirsch in a defeatist gesture. "I'm done."

Hirsch raised his voice. "It is there. I know it. Please, Garand, reconsider. For both our sakes." He raised a hand in a stopping motion, then put the crutch under his arm and raised himself. "Listen, please. Will you just give it another month? If we have nothing at the end of a month, I will abandon it with you. I swear it. Just give it another chance."

Garand stayed silent for a long moment, considering his partner's state. This was not an act, but an impassioned plea from a man who truly believed there was gold there. Did he himself believe Hirsch was mistaken, or was he just so exhausted that he succumbed to taking the easy way out? At this point, he really wasn't sure, not sure enough to maintain his negative position. Again, he acknowledged his lack of alternatives. If he left, what would he do? Would he return to the wandering life Hirsch had plucked him from? And, if he did, what were his prospects? They were nil. At least here he had a place indoors to sleep. And Hirsch's cooking, while not the best in the world, was certainly not poisoning him. And what if he were wrong? What if there was gold in that shaft and he walked away from it? If he later found out Hirsch was right, all he could do then would be to berate himself for another bad decision taken in haste.

Hirsch remained in that half-standing, half-sitting position, supported by the crutch, for the minutes Garand was silent. Finally, he spoke again. "Garand, will you stay?"

Garand let out a heavy breath and now sought to save face by requesting a condition. "I'll give it another month, as you ask. If we have not uncovered anything in that time, I'm leaving. There'll be no further discussion, now or then."

Hirsch smiled. "Yes, all right. Agreed. And, as soon as you are as convinced as I am of the gold's existence, we will register our claim as equal partners." He lowered himself into the chair.

Garand nodded. "All right, then. One month from today. I hope you're right."

After a night of restlessness, struggling with allowing himself to be swayed from a decision he was certain was correct, Garand rose early and had a quick meal. Using a hunting knife he found in the cabin, he carved a two-inch vertical line in the wooden cabin wall.

"What are you doing with that knife?" Hirsch's harsh query caught Garand in mid-turn, the knife still in his hand. He glanced at the sound to see Hirsch sitting up in bed, a halting expression on his face, his eyes bugging out, fixating on the knife.

"One month, Hirsch. Thirty days to the day. That will help me to keep count." Garand pointed with the knife to the mark.

The statement seemed to calm Hirsch as he relaxed, lying back. He spoke after a second of reflection. "There will be no need to count. You will see."

"I'll keep track just the same." Garand flashed a questioning look. "What did you think I was doing with the knife?"

Hirsch waved a hand. "It does not matter... I was still half-asleep."

Garand studied Hirsch for a moment before passing the situation off. Then he stepped outside into the crisp morning air, and, taking up his tools, he returned to the shaft. There he stayed, steadily working until the cart was full. As he exited the mine to bring the mule from the corral, Hirsch stepped out of the cabin.

Their gazes crossed. Neither spoke, but Garand could not avoid the quizzical look he knew was on his face as Hirsch watched as he walked past.

For several days hence, work continued with only minimal conversation as ruffled feelings took time to slowly mend. Garand continued to mark off the days each morning. In the space of a week, traces of gold ore began showing up in his diggings. For the first time since Garand's arrival, Hirsch employed the smelting apparatus to extract gold. It amounted to no more than a thimbleful, but it was gold all the same.

Hirsch put the pebbles into an empty poke. "This is encouraging,"

Garand was not as impressed. "We'll see if it continues."

Two more days passed. At midday, Hirsch led the mule and cart into the yard to empty it. Having spent the morning excavating deeper into the secondary tunnel, Garand's pickaxe sank into a soft spot just above a rather large irregular shaped stone. With the intention of dislodging the rock, he lifted up on the handle to use the axe head as a pry. A great effort pulled the object from its mooring. As the stone hit the ground next to his foot, something inside the resulting hole caught his eye. Light from the coal oil lamp behind him glinted off something shiny. Needing more light to identify it, he reached for the lamp on the side wall, lifted it away, and brought its light to bear on the opening. He squinted to get a better picture as he placed the lamp on a shelf the removal of the object had created. And there it was. Gold. Raw gold ore. He'd struck the vein. As his excitement grew, he cleared more loose dirt and stones away in a frenzied effort. It was a foot wide at least and three feet long, maybe more. Lord only knew how deep it ran. Further digging would yield the answer to that one, but for now, suffice to say he'd unearthed the secret of the Defiance Mine. "We got it!" His shout went unheard, but no matter. His elation had to be released then and there. Dropping the axe, he trotted through the tunnel to the entrance to see Hirsch working over the rocker box.

"Hirsch! Come quick! You have to see this! You have to see this!"

Garand supported himself with both hands against the tunnel's lead timber, exhausted, as Hirsch, reacting to the call, grabbed his crutch and hauled himself to his feet. He turned as Garand waved a hand at him. "Come on! Come on!"

Hirsch mumbled as he hobbled toward the tunnel. "What is it? Did you hit it?"

Garand, a great grin across his face, continued to wave his hand. "Yes, hurry."

Hirsch joined him. They reentered the tunnel. Garand pointed out the find. Hirsch stopped for a second and rubbed his eyes, as if he didn't believe what he saw. He moved closer, lifting the lamp to focus more light. After a few seconds' observance, he became elated.

"Yes, yes, Garand, you got it. That's it. That is what I have been searching for. I knew it was there." He turned to face Garand, a broad grin on his face. "We're rich, Garand, we're rich."

They both laughed heartily.

Hirsch said through his laughter, "You must admit, I was right."

"I do. You were right. I should never have doubted you."

They laughed some more, even louder.

After several minutes of indulging in their delight, they calmed themselves and caught their breath.

Hirsch took a breath. "Let's spend the rest of the day processing what you have dug out so far. Tomorrow we can get into the vein in earnest."

"I agree. We'll need to clear a better path here before we can get the cart in closer."

Hirsch raised a hand with the index finger pointed up. "First, we should have a drink to celebrate our good fortune."

Garand nodded. "That's a great idea."

They had the drink and did the cleanup which took most of the afternoon. Before quitting for the day, Hirsch backed the mule, hitched to the cart, into the secondary tunnel, ready for use the next morning, then they unhitched the mule and put it up for the night.

"I think we should dig in the morning. I will help where I can. In the afternoon, we should process what we've uncovered."

Garand nodded. "Good idea. That will keep us organized and allow us to keep a tally on what we have."

Over the next two weeks, their labors yielded two large sacks of gold nuggets in addition to the poke Hirsch had when they met.

On a hunch, Garand buried some of the gold at the mine site without telling Hirsch. He hated how easily paranoia creeped up on him, but he wanted to remain cautious in case anything happened.

During dinner that night, Hirsch voiced his desire to register the claim as early as the next day. "The sooner we do, the safer we will be. I have a strange feeling someone may be lurking around. Besides, a formal claim will allow us to open a bank account and to hire laborers. We also need to purchase better equipment. We will kill ourselves trying to do this without machines and a crew."

"Well, you've been right about everything else. I've seen nothing out of the ordinary, but, who knows, there could be someone watching us. Plenty of hiding places around here. And I definitely agree about needing help."

"I've seen nothing either. It is just a feeling I have, but it makes sense to be certain we have legal claim. We can leave for Colinas de Oro after breakfast and be back before nightfall."

"Absolutely."

That night, Garand lay on his cot awaiting sleep, but none came. He couldn't explain it, but, for some reason, he could not doze off. It was quiet enough with only the soft sound of Hirsch's measured breathing heard. That was not enough to keep him awake. He was certainly tired enough. Maybe it was the excitement of the find hanging on. After several hours of restlessness, he gave up the wait and flung back the blanket. He rose, and, in underwear in need of washing, he pulled on his clothes and shoes and tiptoed to the door to let himself out of the cabin. Maybe a walk might induce sleep. He moved into the center of the yard between the cabin and the processing equipment and stood there for a moment, staring up at the bright full moon.

Something snapped behind him, a twig maybe, causing him to turn. In front of him, Hirsch stood leaning on his crutch with a revolver in his hand. "What are you doing, Garand? Where are you going?"

Surprised, Garand hesitated. "I… nowhere. I'm not going anywhere. I couldn't sleep. I thought a walk might help."

Hirsch glared at him, shaking his head. "I don't believe you. On the night before we go to register our claim, you can't sleep? Of all the nights—you go off on your own in the middle of the night? You're going to file the claim on your own, aren't you? You're cutting me out. You're nothing but a claim jumper."

"Hirsch, don't be a fool. That idea never occurred to me. I simply couldn't sleep. That's the only reason I'm out here."

Hirsch became incensed. "You're a liar. You're cutting me out. That is why you had that knife. You were considering killing me then, but you needed me to find the gold. Now you don't." He had reached shouting level by the time he'd finished. The look in his eyes had more than anger behind them. They added to the unhinged expression on his face and the ranting in his voice.

Garand shouted back. "Nonsense."

"You're dressed, ready to leave. Why would you be dressed in the middle of the night?"

"I'm dressed because there's a chill in the air. I don't need to get sick."

Hirsch swiped his hand in a negative gesture. "I don't believe you."

Garand took a step closer.

"Stay back. I have a gun."

"Come on, Hirsch. You don't need that gun. I'm no danger to you."

"Stay away."

Garand took another step. "Put the gun away. Let's talk this out. We're partners, you said so yourself. We share equally. I'm good with that. I'm satisfied with that."

Hirsch shrank back. "No. Stay back. I'll shoot you."

"Hirsch, you're being unreasonable. Give me that gun before you hurt yourself. We'll forget this ever happened."

Hirsch raised the gun and cocked its. Garand's mind raced. What was wrong with the man? Had he lost his mind? Had his own greed caused him to think the worst? He had to get the gun away from him before it went off. Once he disarmed him, he could try to calm him and convince him he was mistaken. He reached out.

Hirsch's finger jerked the trigger. The hammer fell, but there was only a click. Somehow, the gun failed. But that click caused something in Garand's mind to snap. Hirsch had just tried to kill him. Reflex action moved him, took him over. He lunged forward, shoving the gun away and grabbing Hirsch's throat. Hirsch fell back, losing balance, as the crutch slid away. Garand's hand brushed the crutch, seemingly suspended in midair, gripping it as Hirsch dropped to the ground. Lifting the crutch above his head, Garand slammed it down hard on Hirsch's body. Hirsch tried to shield himself with his hands as he cried out in pain, fueling the fire in Garand's being. Repeatedly, he lifted and swung the crutch, striking the head several times and landing more blows on the body. Control of his reason was lost as he repeatedly struck out at the perceived threat, grunting and shouting indiscernibly. Finally, Hirsch's cries stopped. His movement stopped. Garand dropped the crutch and collapsed to a knee, breathing heavily from the expended effort.

For a long moment, he stared at Hirsch's motionless body. Blood oozed from several nasty wounds on the head. More came from points on the upper body, all caused by the crutch. No, all caused by his own senseless wielding of that crutch. What had he done? His mind raced over the events of the past few minutes. He'd reacted violently to an aggressive attack by a crazed individual who'd gotten it wrong but had proceeded anyway. Was he justified in his defense? Yes. His life had been threatened, and he'd reacted accordingly. But was he justified in the degree of violence he'd brought to bear? No. His superior strength and agility would have been sufficient to disarm the man and force him to listen. Instead, he allowed anger to take hold of him, to control him, to continue striking out until that which he now stared down at had resulted. There was no excuse for it, no explaining it away. It was wrong, but it was done.

Was Hirsch dead? The question came as Garand berated himself for the amount of brutality he'd delivered. Was it possible that he'd killed his partner? He had to check. Leaning in, he reached to Hirsch's hand to feel for a pulse. Nothing. Dead. Oh, God, Hirsch was dead at his hand. Would this be considered murder? Of course it was self-defense, but was this degree necessary? Absolutely not. A simple swat of his hand would have sufficed. Granted there were no witnesses, but still....

Reality halted his reverie as he leaned back on his haunches. What was he to do? Report this to the authorities? Under normal circumstances, that should be his next move. But his experiences with the police force, or rather the lack of one, in this godforsaken land did not bode well for following the moral path, not if he valued his neck. He'd be in a noose before he knew what was happening.

He shook his head sharply to engage the thought process. Alone here, his actions had not been observed. If he cleaned this mess up, no one would ever be the wiser. It was conceivable no one knew they were working this mine together. If anyone did question Hirsch's whereabouts, which he doubted, he could simply say Hirsch had soured on the existence of gold in the mine and moved on before the vein was uncovered.

Garand moved quickly. Picking up the gun that lay beside Hirsch's body, he examined it carefully, curious why it had not fired. It was loaded and capped, but a good amount of rust was present. It looked as if it had not been cleaned for ages. Maybe the powder had gotten wet or the caps were faulty. Whatever the reason, its failure saved his life. He'd keep the thing. Maybe at another time, he'd try to restore it, but for now, he shoved it into his waistband and turned his attention to Hirsch's body.

A grave would be needed, in a spot out of the way, so if he did bring people in to work the mine, it would not be visible. He dragged the body to a spot behind the cabin at the base of the hill. There he dug out a shallow grave, rolled Hirsch's remains into it, placed the bloody crutch beside it, and packed dirt in to level it with the surrounding ground. The excess earth he sprinkled away in several directions. By the time he'd finished, dawn broke over the area. Garand made a decision—The Defiance was his now, by default if by nothing else. He had the knowledge to work it, if not the wherewithal. That would come with further consideration, but the time had come to register the claim, to assume legal ownership before anything else stood in his way.

4

THE DARK, ALMOST BLACK HORSE Lon called Gray bore him up the street toward the hotel, leading Rhiann's bay horse and a loaded pack mule. They stopped at the hitch rail as Rhiann emerged from the hotel in riding clothes, carrying a carpetbag. Lon flashed a broad grin. She grinned back, and, stepping into the street beside the mule, she lashed the bag to the pack saddle.

Lon removed his hat. "Well now, Miss Swayze, you about ready to head for a Mexican wedding?"

Rhiann smiled as she took the reins from him and mounted. "I am, Mister Pearce."

He replaced the hat. "All right, then, let's head out."

They set out heading south to backtrack the route they had followed from Mexico only a short time earlier. The incidents that had transpired after that trip had drastically changed both their lives. Now they were in the process of taking steps that would ultimately transform them forever. Rhiann wore a smile of anticipation.

Lon set a leisurely pace. Cooler weather coming on made traveling less of a chore. There was no rush and no reason to wear themselves or the stock out. "We'll get there when we get there. It'll be hot thereabouts, don't matter when."

"Where will we cross the river?" Rhiann's question had apprehension in it. She'd almost drowned last time and did not look forward to a second crossing.

"Got no intention a crossing that bear again. We'll head straight south. They's a bridge crosses the Rio Grande at El Paso. Puts us in Mexico a mite longer, but without we get wet. We can resupply at Fort Bliss close by 'fore we cross."

"I like that plan much better." Rhiann cracked a broad smile, which Lon matched.

"Yes, ma'am, I reckoned you would."

Rhiann shook her head. Yes, ma'am, indeed. But that was one of the things she loved about Lon, his respectful, sometimes playful way.

The first few days were a pleasant, uneventful ride. Lon's Winchester took down several small animals. Each camp afforded a good hot meal and the promise of a good night's sleep under the stars. As they had lain in their bedrolls on the first night, counting the stars in a clear moonlit sky, a thought had occurred to Rhiann.

"Should we keep guard through the night?"

"Naw, you rest easy. Gray'll hear something coming a mile away."

Close enough to lean over to him, she turned his head and kissed him tenderly. He responded gently.

"Goodnight, Lon."

"Night, Rhiann."

About a week out, leaving the white sands southeast of Albuquerque and entering the mountains, they found themselves slowed by the steady ascent. They relied on Gray's sure-footedness and ability to sense danger in enough time for them to react. As they climbed a steep grade, Gray slowed and shook his head, mane flowing in the hefty breeze. A low whinny accompanying the move took Lon's attention. He patted the horse's neck.

"Good boy, Gray." He turned to Rhiann, who'd stopped beside him. "We got company somewheres close by. Keep a sharp eye peeled."

"What do think it might be?"

"Not sure. Likely four-legged. Gray don't act up like that to two-leggeds less'n they got bad intentions. Two-leggeds don't keep hid as good neither. We'll just mosey on, careful-like."

Lon pulled the Winchester from its saddle scabbard and set it across the saddle behind the horn. "Stay close."

They moved on with the pack mule in tow, Rhiann riding close either beside Lon or behind him when the path narrowed. As they entered a pass flanked on either side by abruptly rising rock walls, Gray reacted again, this time stopping completely.

Lon scanned the leveling path ahead, then the walls. Rhiann added her sight to the scan. Neither saw anything, but, in the distance, a high pitched growl could be heard, causing a further stirring from Gray.

"All right, easy, boy, I hear it. It's up ahead, pretty high, can't tell which side."

Rhiann drew the revolver from her hip holster. "I'll watch the left."

Lon levered a round into the rifle's chamber. "Go real slow. I'll watch this side. Easy now. Get on, Gray."

The horse moved forward hesitantly. Rhiann stayed close. Scanning both walls, they relied on the horses to stay on path. Rhiann's horse stayed close to Gray. The barriers stayed consistent for an eighth of a mile before tapering down toward the pass floor. Slowly they approached the end of the corridor, an open area.

Gray suddenly stopped and turned slightly, grunting, head pulling sharply to the right and back. Lon shifted in the saddle to afford a view of the wall behind him. Rhiann guessed the reaction was some mystical connection between horse and rider, Lon reading the meaning of Gray's action. Lon hastily raised the Winchester to his shoulder and sighted on a golden blur rapidly descending in midair from the rocks above. Rhiann's eyes made the blur out to be a big cat as the scene played out almost in slow motion. She glanced at Lon as he pulled the rifle's trigger. The crack shattered the quiet as the round plucked the cat from its downward path at the midpoint. Twisted and flipped by the force of the bullet, it thumped heavily on the pass floor behind them, still moving. Quickly, expertly, Lon levered another round in place and fired the final kill shot. The slug hit its mark in the cat's chest area. No further movement occurred.

Lon held sight on the body for a long moment, then lowered the rifle and emitted a heavy breath. Rhiann, in awe of his snap-shot accuracy, watched him dismount and step out from between the horses.

The pack mule, lashed to Lon's saddle horn, made uneasy movements and let out snorts as Lon walked past it toward the felled cat. Cautiously, he inserted a boot toe under the carcass and shoved it slightly, keeping the Winchester trained on it. Then he turned, lowering the rifle, and walked back to Rhiann.

"Mountain lion. Dead. We'll leave him here to draw any other animals in the area. Likely be quiet for a spell."

"How did you do that?"

"What, the shot?"

She nodded quickly, still in shock.

He smiled. "I didn't get him, he'd a got the mule, likely us too." He shrugged. "So I got him."

She laughed nervously. "I don't know how you can make it sound so easy, but I'm very glad you did it." She holstered her sidearm.

"Yeah, well, me too." He remounted and shoved the Winchester back in its holster.

They moved on.

COMING OUT OF THE HILL country onto the flatter plains southeast of Las Cruces, they spent their last night on the trail before reaching Fort Bliss slightly south of the New Mexico/Texas border. The temperature had already risen dramatically compared to up north. Lower altitudes on the plains increased that intensity. Toward the end of the day, Lon picked a site that backed up to a clump of boulders. With that at their back, there would be only three sides to watch. At dusk, they picketed and cared for the animals, set up camp, and cooked the last of their hunt stores for supper.

"We'll make Fort Bliss by midday," Lon said across the fire. "El Paso's just a mite west of the fort."

"You know, I wouldn't mind staying over in El Paso. We could both use a bath and a comfortable bed even if it is only one night."

Lon nodded. "Yeah, reckon so."

Rhiann got up and walked to where her saddle lay on the ground. She released the blanket roll and spread it out. "Tonight we have the stars for our ceiling."

Lon rose and went to her. He put his arms around her. "You some kinda poet or something?"

She smiled. "Not that I know of."

"Surely sounds like it. Reckon you're saying you're good with being out here."

"As long as I'm with you." She kissed him, a long, lingering kiss, and let out a tiny whimper as he pulled her tight against him. She leaned away and sank into his embrace.

He whispered in her ear. "You surely are a tempting woman, Miss Rhiann Swayze."

She whispered back. "I'm not fighting you off."

"I know, but you won't have to. You're worth the wait in gold."

She chuckled. "Now who's the poet?" She kissed him again.

They slept soundly, tired from a long day in a hard journey. Crickets and owls and various nocturnal creatures sang a distant song as their relaxed, measured breaths seemed in unison.

LON ROLLED SLIGHTLY IN HIS blanket. Gray's nickers settled in his ear, causing him to open his eyes. He'd been in this situation before. Gray's sounds meant they had company. Unwanted company. He remained quiet and listened. Gray nickered again. Staying low, Lon folded the blanket back and lifted the Colt from its holster draped on the saddle horn. He reached silently across the few inches between him and Rhiann and placed his hand over her mouth. She was instantly awake.

"Shh. Company. Don't move."

She nodded.

He removed his hand and made a motion for her to stay put. Rolling out of the blanket, he went to a low crawl in the direction of the picket line. Squirming his way to Gray, he came to a crouch and reached up to pat the horse's nose. Hidden in the shadows, he waited.

A minute later, two figures moved cautiously into the camp. Their outlines were framed by the low light from the dwindling fire. They walked past the picket line toward the blanket rolls that lay close to the fire. They were big men. Both moved with their hands resting on their side arms.

Lon rose and took one step forward, taking the animals out of the line of fire. He leveled his weapon. "Freeze, gents. You ain't welcome here."

Both men froze. Each shot a fleeting glance at the other.

"Now, with one hand, unbuckle them shell belts and let 'em drop."

Neither moved.

Lon cocked the Colt slowly, letting the clicks sink in. "Do it!"

One man turned his head slightly to call over his shoulder. "Or how about we just draw down on you? You can't get but one of us, maybe. T'other'll get you, sure as hell."

"You'll die for the trying."

They stood still.

Then another voice joined in. "Or how about we just even the odds?" Rhiann stood across the fire, her Colt Lightning leveled on them. "Now you're caught in a crossfire, in case you haven't noticed, so do as the man tells you. Shed your guns." Her voice, while a bit jittery, still had authority behind it.

The decision having been made for them, the intruders had no choice but to comply. The gun belts hit the ground in a clump.

Lon wasn't finished. "Kick 'em away."

They did it, then Lon moved in, keeping his distance. "Raise your hands and get on over to the fire." They complied, moving slowly to stand in the flickering campfire light.

Rhiann stayed put. "That's far enough."

In the yellowish tint of the firelight, they were big and slovenly, in grimy clothes and floppy hats. Their whiskered faces were filthy, and the smell emanating from them nearly overpowered her.

Lon stepped in behind them, keeping a bead on them.

"Lon, think what you're doing." Rhiann's words brought him up short. "Remember Santa Fe."

She'd all but told him what he must not do. He took a moment. This had to come out without killing these idjits, as much as they deserved it. Then he had his plan. "Take off your boots."

"What?" This came from the man who'd spoken earlier.

"I said get your boots off. Now."

That moved them. One man simply kicked off ill-fitting boots. The other had to struggle to lift each leg, pulling his boots off.

Lon glanced at Rhiann. "Keep 'em covered a minute."

Rhiann nodded.

Lon squatted and rummaged in his saddlebag to pull out two lengths of rope. Lowering the hammer on his revolver, he stuck it into his waistband to free up both hands. Roughly, he pulled one man's hands behind his back and tied them in place. He did the same with the other, then produced and cocked his gun.

"Now start walking."

"You can't—"

"Get yonder of this camp. Hell, get out of these parts altogether. Show up here again, you'll be chewing lead 'fore you know it's coming."

Grumbling, they turned and walked gingerly on bare feet over rough terrain, trying to balance themselves without their arms to stabilize them. A few ouches came from them as they stumbled into the night.

Lon relaxed the hammer as he crossed quickly to where Rhiann maintained her stance, her gun still in position to fire. He noticed her hand trembling slightly and the intense expression on her face. She seemed distant. "Rhiann, you all right?"

She turned her head slightly toward him. "Yeah… yeah, it's just… that reminded me of—"

His arms reached out. He took hold of her shoulders in a securing gesture. He guessed she'd relived the confrontation with Logan Yaeger only a short time earlier. It'd been her first kill, and it unnerved her something fierce. "I know. I shouldn't never put you in that spot again." The event was as vivid in his mind as he knew it was in hers. She didn't need reminding by these varmints.

She lowered her weapon. "No, it's not your fault. I agreed to this. I knew full well something like this might happen. That part was hard, but I was more worried about you, what you might do."

He shook his head. "Don't be. I learn pretty quick, just maybe got to be brought up short a time or two. You can put up that iron now. They won't be coming back."

She looked at him. "Are you sure?"

He smiled. "They're hogtied and bootless. Would you?"

She dropped the gun on her bedroll and embraced him.

He hugged her back and whispered to her. "What do you say we get some sleep? Big day tomorrow."

She held on tighter. "Mmmm. Just hold me for a bit first."

AFTER A RESTLESS SLEEP, THEY rose early and got back on the trail quickly, making Fort Bliss by mid-morning on a clear day that promised oppressive heat. The image of the fort surprised Rhiann as they stopped to observe it from a distance.

"That looks more like a town than a fort"

"Yup. Never could cipher what they was thinking."

They moved on and were permitted unrestricted entry. There were no walls or parapets, no gun emplacements, no guards. The prominent parade grounds, covering the full expanse of the installation, though empty at the moment, displayed the capacity for training and pageantry it could provide. Behind it, two large houses provided officer accommodations. The enlisted men's barracks and the various buildings that made up the crux of the operation were tucked beyond, all but hidden.

Their stay was short, taking only enough time to make the purchases that replenished their dwindling supplies. Then they moved west the few miles to El Paso.

"Changed a mite since the last time I come through here. Got considerable bigger." He guided Rhiann down St. Louis Street to the imposing Grand Central Hotel, beside an impressive square block of carefully maintained gardens. They dismounted in front and beat the Texas dust from their clothes. Rhiann released her carpetbag from the ties on the mule's rigging and carried it in. A starch-collared clerk greeted them at the front desk.

"How do?" Lon's greeting was pleasant if not weary. "We'd like two rooms for the night."

"Travelers, I'd say." The clerk made the observation as he turned the register book to face them. His drawn, mustached face seemed hungry for knowledge of his new guests. "Not married then?"

Lon picked up the pencil in the centerfold of the book. "Just travelers." He spoke in a matter of fact tone, looking the clerk squarely in the eye. "The rest's our business and none a yourn."

A sheepish look crossed the clerk's face. "Of course, sir."

Lon signed the register using his given name, Alonzo Pearce. He noted this was the first time since he'd taken to the outlaw trail that using his own name was possible without concern for putting himself in danger. He handed the pencil to Rhiann.

As she signed, she pointed to his name and glanced at him. "Feels good, doesn't it?"

Lon smiled. "Yes, ma'am." He directed his attention to the clerk. "Where can I put up the stock?"

The clerk seemed confused. "Sir?"

Rhiann leaned in. "Where can we board our horses?" She said it slowly, likely to make it clear.

"Oh, sure. There's a full stable behind the hotel."

Lon nodded. "Thanks. How much?"

"Two dollars."

Rhiann dropped two silver dollars on the counter. The clerk picked them up, then hesitated, a puzzled expression on his face.

Rhiann looked at him. "Is there a problem?"

He quickly recovered. "No, ma'am, not at all." He fumbled to get the keys to adjoining rooms on the third floor and handed them over. "Luggage?"

Rhiann lifted the carpetbag. "I can handle it."

Lon led her to the staircase to their right, and they started up. At Rhiann's room, Lon unlocked the door and opened it.

"You go ahead on and get settled in. I'll take care of the stock."

She hesitated. "I can help."

Lon smiled. "No need. Won't take long."

She kissed him quickly and stepped inside.

The hotel's dining room proved equal to the establishment's high standards. For the first time in weeks, they ate well. Returning to the rooms, they were both stuffed and slightly affected by the wine they'd consumed. It took a good amount of control for Lon to maintain his promise of hands off until marriage. True to his word, he managed it.

"Thank you for a lovely evening, Mister Pearce." There was a sing-song cadence to Rhiann's voice.

"You are very welcome, Miss Swayze."

A long kiss in the hallway sealed the evening.

5

GARAND PACED IN FRONT OF the cabin, several days after the fatal encounter, undecided how to proceed. The time had come to register his claim to the Defiance, but the details had to be worked out. Should he ride Hirsch's mule into Colinas de Oro, or should he walk? It was hot and humid, and riding beat walking by a mile. Hirsch would certainly not need the mule any longer, but would the mule raise questions? Garand had his story planned out in case curious people asked the whereabouts of the gimpy old foreigner.

He directed the mule down the single dirt street to the sign suspended over an office across from Taylor's Saloon. The sign read, *Assays and Claims.* The free standing building was almost tiny, with a plate glass front window, the lettering on which stated the same as the sign, but underneath, the addition of another line, *Stuart Flick, Certified Assayer.* The entrance door was beside the window. Visible inside, a tall, slim, bald man stood at a counter that contained a fairly large brass balance scale. Garand dismounted and tied the mule off on a metal ring attached to a post driven into the ground in front of the low porch.

He went to the door and opened it, hesitating in the doorway as the man inside looked up. Garand walked to the counter, noting Flick's height—over six feet—and his somewhat stooped posture. His long face had a meticulously groomed van dyke hair growth, and he wore a collarless white shirt and a dark vest that partially concealed sporty red suspenders.

"Can I help you?" His voice was deep but without much authority.

Garand reached inside his shirt and pulled out a small leather poke. "I want to file a claim." He dropped the poke on the counter. "This is a sample from it."

Flick opened the drawer string. He lifted out a nugget and dropped it in his palm to scrutinize it. "Isn't that Hirch's mule?" he asked as he studied the nugget with definite interest.

And there it was. It had to happen sooner or later, and he'd have to respond.

"It was, but he abandoned it." Garand recited his story as he'd rehearsed it. "Our efforts to find the gold in the mines hadn't paid off yet, and he lost hope and wandered off who knows where. I stayed on a hunch, and after a few more days of digging, I struck the vein. By then, Hirsch was long gone."

"Ain't that a shame." Flick placed the nugget on one of the scale pans. "Pretty pure from the look of it. I'll have to assay it to be sure before I can register the claim."

"How long will that take?" Garand eyed the poke protectively.

"Oh, several hours. You might want to get a meal or something while you wait." Flick gestured to the saloon across the street. "Taylor's over there has fairly good food."

"Yes, I know. If it's all the same to you, I'll just wait here."

Flick shrugged. "Up to you." He picked up the sack and shook a few pieces onto the scale pan. "There. That should be enough for the assay." He pulled the drawstring to close the poke and handed it back to Garand. Then, lifting the brass pan off the scale, he turned for a door behind him and slipped into the back room.

As the door closed, Garand went to the bench that spanned the length of the window and sat, pushing the poke inside his shirt. He bided his time uncomfortably for what seemed like an hour while Flick remained in the other room. Slight clattering sounds came from there, which Garand attributed to the assay process, although he had no knowledge of the procedure.

The door opened abruptly, and Flick slipped out, closing and locking it in a clandestine manner. Appearing nervous, he hurried to the front door. "While that's processing, there's an errand I forgot to run. I'll be back in a few minutes." It was obviously directed at Garand, but Flick's gaze stayed straight ahead. He failed to take his hat as he stepped out nervously.

Garand watched as Flick quickly left the office. He found Flick's actions a bit strange but passed it off as either a sudden remembrance of the errand or merely a quirk. Giving it no further concern, he continued to wait uneasily, first tapping a foot, then pacing, then retaking his seat, folding and unfolding his arms. Nothing worked to settle him down.

Flick was gone for longer than what Garand considered "a few minutes." Garand sat fidgeting, shifting on the bench. This was taking way too long. What the hell kind of errand was so important for him to interrupt his work? Did this have something to do with Hirsch's disappearance? After all, Hirsch was known in town. He'd spent time searching out a partner, probably quite vocally. Now, for him to be absent while the claim was registered might have generated questions for which Flick sought answers.

Garand's heart rate increased, his breathing becoming short. He took deep breaths to calm himself. He had to maintain appearances for this to work. Slowly, his breathing exercises settled him, but his disease with a situation he could not control remained, troubling him.

He looked around as the door opened to see Flick enter, much calmer than he'd been when he left. Crossing quickly to the back door, Flick unlocked it and entered stealthily. Garand watched as the door closed. *What the hell is going on with him?*

In a few minutes, Flick, a sheet of paper in hand and a broad smile on his face, stepped out and came to stand in front of Garand. "This is one of the purest samples I've ever seen. It equates to sixteen ounces to the ton." He handed Garand the sheet.

Garand looked the page over, not understanding the numbers scribbled next to the printed symbols of metals contained in the sample. The result scrawled at the bottom left nothing to the imagination. Garand grinned. "I guess I can register the claim now, huh?"

Flick's expression became businesslike. "Not quite yet. I'm required to verify the exact location and size of the claim and to make sure it doesn't infringe on anyone else's claim. I'll have to do a physical inspection."

Garand hesitated. "I had no idea this was so involved."

"Legal requirement. Look at it like buying a house. You'd have to do a survey before the sale can go through to make sure the house and the land are what they purport to be. This is almost exactly the same thing."

That made sense to Garand. This had to be legal and binding so he could get into developing the mine without concerns. "Yeah, I can see that. We can go now if you'd like."

Flick nodded. He took the dark, narrow brimmed felt hat from the hat tree and put it on. "Exactly my thought. I have a friend bringing my horse around." He looked out the window. "I see you already have transportation."

Garand chuckled. "Not as elegant as yours, I'd say, but serviceable."

Flick flashed a curious look. "Strange Hirsch walked off without taking his mule. As I recall, he depended on the mule for transportation, being crippled and all."

Garand shrugged. Shit, no, don't bring that up. "I don't know. The last few days before he left, he acted really strange. I couldn't figure out what was going on with him."

"Yeah, well, folks *do* say he's a little off in the head. No matter, though. Let's go."

Garand got up as Flick opened the door. They stepped out. Flick produced a key and locked it, then glanced up the street. "Here's my friend coming now."

Garand looked in the direction Flick indicated to see a slim, fully bearded individual in a white shirt and the vest and trousers of a dark suit but without the jacket. Wearing a wide brimmed straw hat, he led two saddled horses. Garand's first question, one he didn't ask, was, why two horses? The second, also not asked, was who was this person?

The man reached them in a few seconds, stopping beside Flick. He was about half a head shorter than Flick. Garand noticed the badge pinned to his vest. Flick gestured to the man. "This is Deputy Sheriff Strome."

That was confusing. The presence of a law officer put Garand off, but he'd better play along. He reached out a hand. "Victor Garand." They shook hands.

Strome showed an interested look on his round, somewhat pudgy face. "Say, I seen you in town a while back, didn't I? You were with that old coot, the foreigner, right? Where's he at?"

Not again. "I don't know. He convinced me to partner up with him on this mine he'd been working. He swore there was gold there.'" He once more relayed the story he'd given Flick of Hirsch wandering off without even taking his mule.

"The same mine your sample came from?" Strome asked.

"As a matter of fact, it is. I figured I'd better get it registered now." Strome looked concerned. "Without your partner?"

"If he comes back, I'll definitely cut him in, half and half," Garand assured him. "After all, it was his idea from the start."

Flick moved toward his horse. "Well, I'd say that's damn nice of you since he walked out on you." He looked over at Strome. "Ready?"

Strome nodded.

Flick took the reins from him. "What do you say we get going?" He seemed impatient now.

"Is there a reason the deputy is coming?"

Flick swung up into the saddle. "Why, Reuben will be your witness to the claim's authenticity. Besides, you never know what might be lurking out there. Wild country, you know. We might just need his protection."

Unconvinced, Garand shrugged, letting it go and mounting the mule. They started out.

GARAND LED THE WAY BACK to the mine site with Flick and Strome riding together behind. The conversation was hushed behind him, their voices just loud enough for Garand to hear, but not enough to understand their words. They were either friends and had subjects of their own to discuss, or his rising suspicion that something else was going on here was credible. He would have to let this play out to learn which was true. To blurt out his skepticism now would only cause problems where perhaps none existed.

They rode onto the property. Garand stopped the mule at the corral gate and slid off. Flick and Strome drew up beside him and dismounted, lashing their mounts to the top corral rail. Garand questioned to Flick. "What's next?"

"Can you show us the vein you struck?"

Garand waved them forward. "The shaft." He lead the way to the tunneled opening and lifted a kerosene lamp from a nail in the support timber.

"Is it safe?" This came from Strome as he pushed on a timber.

"It hasn't collapsed on me yet," Garand's stated with sarcasm. He was tired of this intrusion.

They entered as Garand struck a match and lit the lamp. It threw enough light to allow them to find the end of the tunnel. Garand held the lamp up to shine on the vein, almost glowing in the yellow light.

Flick stepped up and touched the area, somewhat reverently. Garand thought the act a bit odd, but he let it pass.

Flick said nothing more. He and Strome turned and walked out. Garand followed, extinguishing the lamp and replacing it on its nail.

Flick glanced around the area. "I've got to walk the perimeter and check for any neighboring properties."

"There's nothing but hills back there." Garand indicated the back wall that bore the tunnel opening. "Nothing on either side for a good mile all around, but you're welcome to walk it off if you like."

Flick nodded. "Yeah, I'll have to do that. Walk with me, Reuben. Garand, stay where we can find you."

"Sure, I'll be right here."

Flick led off with Strome following. Together they inspected the equipment, then climbed along a rough path leading to the crest of a tall hill above where the equipment was set. They all but disappeared as they reached the top.

Garand stood by, his hands clasped behind his back idly. He paced a little. The inspection of that side took a quarter hour. When they returned, Flick had a question.

"What's up there?" He pointed to the opposite slope rising steeply behind the cabin.

"Just more mountain. As near as I can figure, this is all part of a natural chasm that's probably been here for ages. It all leads to the top way up there." He pointed to the pinnacle of the mountain mass that made up the back wall above the mine shaft. "And goes on for miles."

"Well, we'll have to check it. Is there a way up?"

"There's a path behind the cabin. It winds around. I'd be careful."

Strome called over his shoulder as they made their way around the cabin. "We will."

Garand clasped his hands behind his back again and paced a bit more. He was not comfortable with them being in such close proximity with Hirsch's grave. After a few moments, a call reached him.

"Hey, Garand, come on back here." It was Strome's voice and not a request. Apprehensive, Garand complied, walking to the rear of the cabin.

Flick and Strome stood beside the section of freshly turned earth, devoid of grass.

Strome pointed to it. "What's this?"

Garand stopped short and thought fast. "I, eh, I killed a big cat the other day. I buried it there to keep the vermin from snooping around."

Strome's hands went to his hips. "Big cat, huh? Looks more the size of a man."

"I, eh—"

"Let's have a look at this cat."

"What?" A chill ran up Garand's spine. No, not that.

"You heard me. Dig it up." Strome pointed to the cabin wall. "Shovel right there. Dig it up. Let's see."

Garand froze in place.

"I just gave you a legal order, Garand. Dig it up!"

Garand tried to wiggle out of it. "It's just a cat, that's all. You've got no right—"

"I told you to dig it up. If you refuse, that's resisting an officer of the law. That won't go well for you. Now, do what I tell you."

Shit! He was caught.

Either way, obeying or disobeying, Hirsch's body would be revealed, and that would mean consequences. Reluctantly, with no way around it, he grabbed the shovel and started digging.

"Wait a minute. What's that?" Strome pointed to the newly un-covered branch, the blood stained branch Hirsch used as a crutch. Garand stopped dead, staying silent.

"Never mind. Keep digging."

Garand complied, soon unearthing the entire branch and part of the body, a small part but enough to see it was a man. More digging revealed the identity.

Strome leaned in for a closer look. "Son of a bitch.'" His sidearm came out, pointing at Garand. "Big cat, my ass. That's the foreigner. And that branch? That's his crutch. I recognize it now."

Garand raised his hands, palms out, in a negative gesture. "You don't understand. He attacked me. For no reason at all, he attacked me like a crazy man. I had to defend myself."

Strome took a step back, out of reach of the shovel. Flick moved away, staying in the background.

"We'll get to that." Strome waved a hand at the shovel. "Keep digging. Let's see all of this crazy-man attacker of yours."

Garand continued scraping earth away until Hirsch's mangled body was laid bare. Strome studied it carefully for several minutes.

"So you say he attacked you. What did he use, that branch? Then why don't you have any marks on you? That's his blood, right?"

"He... he had a gun." Garand shifted about, nervously. Maybe mentioning the weapon would even the sizes between himself and Hirsch.

"Did he shoot you?"

"He tried, but it didn't fire."

"What happened to the gun?"

Garand thought quickly. "I threw it away. I don't like guns."

Strome pressed the point. "Did you shoot him?"

"No, I don't have a gun. I told you, I don't like them."

"So, what, you beat him to death?"

"I had to defend myself. He was... he was like a crazy man."

Strome was silent for a few seconds. He tugged at his chin as he pondered. "I'll tell you what I think happened. You two fought over the gold in that shaft over there. Maybe you were going to file alone and cut him out and he figured that out. Or maybe you couldn't agree on the split. Whatever the reason, you beat the living shit out of him, probably with that branch, and then buried him back here so nobody'd know. I've seen it countless times in the gold fields, partners fall out, one kills the other."

Garand's voice went up an octave. "No, it was self-defense."

"Self-defense, my ass. Look at the size of the man and the size of you. You could a put him away with one punch, but, no, you had to keep wailing on him till he was a bloody mess and dead."

"It wasn't like that." Garand was shouting now, almost pleading. "You don't understand—"

"No, you don't understand. What you did to this poor bastard wasn't self-defense, it was murder plain and simple, and it won't stand in my jurisdiction. You're under arrest, Garand."

"No, you have to listen to me."

"I'm done listening, and you're done lying. Get on over to that mule. You're going to jail."

6

TWO GRUELING DAYS IN THE hot Mexican sun brought Lon and Rhiann closer to the mission. As they topped a rise and started down a steep grade, Lon took in the panoramic view. "We're close. Commencing to look familiar."

Rhiann saw no difference. "How can you tell?"

Lon waved a hand. "Them's the mountains I hid out at."

Rhiann looked but still saw nothing recognizable. She shrugged. "If you say so."

As they reached more level ground, Rhiann's mount dropped back, favoring one foreleg. It quickly became a limp. "Lon…." Her voice went up in apprehension. This couldn't be good.

Lon pulled Gray up and turned toward Rhiann as her mount continued to limp forward. "Hold 'im up. Let's have a look-see."

Rhiann pulled rein. The horse stopped, head hung, and immediately raised the leg to take pressure off an obviously offending hoof, balancing on three legs.

Lon dismounted and hurried to them. He crouched at the leg and reached to steady it. The horse shied. "Whoa, son, easy." He reached again. Another shrink back, accompanied by a frightened whinny. Then Gray let out two low nickers, calming the horse.

Again, Rhiann marveled at Gray's ability to communicate. She shook her head, almost in disbelief as Lon caught the hoof for a closer look.

"Yep. There it is," he said.

"What?"

"Stone. Wedged 'twixt the shoe and inside the hoof." He pulled out a pocket knife and used it to loosen the object. After a tense few seconds of probing, a final flick unseated it. Lon leaned back. "There you go. Good as new."

The horse set hoof to ground and tentatively put weight on it. Confident, the horse's head came up, ready to move.

Lon stood up as Rhiann leaned forward. "You two are amazing."

Lon grinned, shaking his head. "Nah, just experienced is all."

Another day's travel put them within sight of the mission. An imposing complex of ten-foot-high adobe walls, it was large enough to be visible from a mile away even through cord grass as tall as a horse's withers. The waning late afternoon sun was a yellow and orange ball that hung in the sky beyond, appearing ready to drop on the mission, casting a coppery tinge to the normally pale gray walls.

"Look yonder." Lon waved a hand toward the huge enclosure.

Rhiann smiled. "Looks good to me."

Tired and dirty, they perked up at the sight and kept moving toward it. As they'd both learned during their separate stays at La Misión de Santa Maria, hers a short few days—his many months—this was more than a church. It had grown to become a village, peopled with the faithful who tended the grounds and lived in the relative safety of the fort-like structure. It was an oasis for those who existed on the outskirts, farming and shepherding and the like. And it was all the responsibility of the benevolent *Padre* Guillermo Cortez, the American priest from New York City who'd long ago found a home here among the peasants.

As Lon had conveyed to Rhiann, *Padre* Cortez had helped him when he first fled to Mexico to escape the lawmen and bounty hunters who hunted him north of the border. Rhiann had gathered bits and pieces of the story allowed by the *padre* when she showed up a few months earlier in her bid to track Lon down. She'd had to convince *Padre* Cortez that her intentions were beneficial to the outlaw, but, once she'd done that, he readily pointed her in the right direction, along with his blessing. An amazing man, this priest with the Mexican name who spoke perfect English.

As they got closer, Lon reached out and took Rhiann's hand. He squeezed it and grinned. She felt a rush up her spine, anticipating the coming events without dwelling on the specifics but trusting that *Padre* Cortez would see them through it. And, hopefully, they'd be able to enjoy the aftermath in some sort of comfort within the mission instead of in saddle blankets under the stars. She smiled back, a warm one with a silent promise of things to come. They continued riding, hand in hand, until the rough Mexican terrain forced them apart.

The tall, solid wood door at the front of the mission had a sign above it in faded, weather worn black paint identifying the location. Screwed into the door, a stout metal plate with a ring the size of two fists acted as a knocker. It was positioned at the height of an average man's shoulder, requiring Lon to lean down from Gray's saddle to announce their presence. His rapping echoed across the plains for several seconds. They waited.

Within moments, scraping came from beyond the door, indicating someone was in the process of opening it. The door swung wide, pushed by an older man in soiled white clothing and a wide brimmed straw hat. He stopped when the door was almost at right angles with the wall, looking up at the visitors. *"Si?"* His voice was soft and gravelly.

Lon let Gray take a step forward. *"Cómo estás?"* His Spanish was perfect, surprising Rhiann.

The man hesitated, studying Lon for a long moment. "Ah, *señor Pearce, y la dama. Sí, sí, entra por favor."*

"Gracias." Lon smiled and heeled Gray gently, dragging the pack

mule behind him. Rhiann followed, interpreting the brief conversation as a greeting and invitation to enter.

As the old man closed the creaking door behind them, they proceeded across the square to the hitch rail outside the church and halted. They dismounted wearily and stood there for a second, stretching their legs and bodies after long hours in the saddle. The old man hurried across to them and, without a word, took their reins, leading the animals toward a nearby stable.

Rhiann smiled as she turned to Lon, thankful for the old man's intervention to assume the chore of caring for the stock. She was tired, and, frankly, the prospect of that bit of work was unpalatable. Lon smiled back, probably of the same thought.

She looked past Lon to see the church door open, allowing a figure in a brown robe to exit. *Padre* Cortez. His face was covered in a white beard as Rhiann remembered from their first meeting. As he stepped out, he covered his bald head with a wide brimmed straw hat, a strip of white hair showing around the sides. Seemingly preoccupied, he barely noticed the visitors until he was almost on top of them. He looked up abruptly, startled. *"Perdóname."*

Lon spoke up. "How do, *Padre?*"

The old priest took a second, then recognition grabbed him. "Alonzo!" There was astonishment in his aging voice.

Lon cracked a broad grin and extended his hand. *Padre* Cortez took the hand and pulled Lon close for a hug. "Oh, my son, it's so good to see you. I've prayed for you." He looked toward Rhiann as he let Lon out of the embrace. "And, Miss...." It appeared his memory failed him momentarily.

Rhiann helped him. "Swayze, *Padre*. But just call me Rhiann." She spoke through a grin.

He took her extended hand in both of his and held it. "Yes, yes, Rhiann, of course. My apologies. The momentary lapse of an old man. My dear, it's so good to see you again." He beamed as he stepped back for a better look at them. "While I've prayed for you both, and for your return, I never thought I would see you again. To what do I owe this pleasure?"

Lon spoke up. "Well, sir, we come to sorta put you to work."

The *padre* stopped with his mouth open, obviously not comprehending. "I… I don't understand."

"We've come to ask you to marry us." Rhiann maintained her grin.

The priest took a second, his mouth still open. His face registered growing awareness as the index finger of his left hand subtly pointed to Lon, then to Rhiann, and back to Lon. "Ah, of course, I see now. Oh, this is more than I could have hoped for. Lovely, lovely. Yes, yes, you must tell me everything that's happened since we last met. We must sit and talk of these things." He was at the point of overflowing.

Lon's smile changed to momentary concern. "You know, ain't neither of us Catholic."

Padre Cortez chuckled. "Catholics are not the only people who marry, my son. And I am well aware that Catholicism is not the only way to heaven. It will be my privilege to help you both become one in marriage."

Rhiann's smile, interrupted by Lon's statement, returned. "We were hoping you'd see it that way."

"I may be a priest, my child, but I'm also a realist. And I appreciate the fact that you've come all this way to allow me to participate in the beginning of your new life together. But come, please, you must freshen up after your journey, then break bread with me and tell me of all your adventures… en *el Norte*."

THE CELL DOOR CLANGED AS it slammed shut. Halfway across the cell floor, Garand recovered from the shove he'd taken as Strome forced him into the cell.

"Circuit judge'll be here next week." Strome turned the key in the lock. "You can cool your heels in there till he comes."

Garand bounded from the center of the cell to the metal bars, grabbing a bar in each hand. "This is ridiculous. I told you it was self-defense."

Strome chuckled. "Yeah, well. Tell it to the judge." He seemed taken with himself over the use of the cliché phrase as he hung the key ring on the opposite clapboard wall and stepped out.

Frustrated, Garand surveyed his circumstances as he looked around the cell at the meager cot against the back wall and the metal pot, for obvious purposes, on the floor nearby. He didn't have much of a chance in here. Iron bars. Locked in. Evidence stacked against him. Well, not really stacked, but read the wrong way, painting him as a murderer. Not true. If he was anything he was an overzealous defender of his own life. But, if the deputy had anything to say about it, and it appeared he had a lot to say, he'd committed the murder of his partner for gain—sole possession of the mine and its gold. No, he didn't have much of a chance, if any at all. All he had was his word, which wouldn't stand for much in a town that didn't know him and didn't appear to care.

This situation would have to change, and he'd have to do the changing. He had a week, maybe less, before the circuit judge would bring him to trial and quickly find him guilty. In that time, he had to come up with some kind of a plan to extricate himself.

He sat heavily on the lumpy, probably pest-infested bunk and, with elbows propped on his knees, dropped his head in his hands. *Think, God damn it, think!*

STROME ENTERED TAYLOR'S SHORTLY AFTER locking up his prisoner. He scanned the sparsely populated saloon.

"Meet me at Taylor's when you're finished," Flick had told him as they parted after bringing Garand to Colinas de Oro in custody. He'd given no reason for the request, which had raised Strome's curiosity.

Flick was seated at a table in a secluded corner. Strome headed that way, determined to satisfy his now aroused interest.

Flick looked up. "Sit down. Have a drink." He gestured to a bottle with an empty glass beside it sitting in the center of the round table.

"Little early for that, wouldn't you say?" Strome noticed the label on the bottle. Not a cheap brand.

"Oh, come on. You just arrested a murderer. Feather in your cap. Calls for a toast. Maybe more than one." Flick uncorked the bottle and poured a generous portion into the glass. He pushed it Strome's way as the deputy sat down across from him.

Strome flashed a grin. "Yeah, I guess so." He lifted the glass and took a sip.

Flick followed suit, leaning in across the table. He spoke softly. "It's probably a safe bet they'll hang that fellow. Do you agree?"

"Well, we've got his confession. You witnessed that. And we've got the body, or what's left of it. I'd say there's a good chance he'll be convicted. Hanging'd be the next step after that."

"How can we… guarantee that?"

That caught Strome off guard. "What?"

Flick leaned closer, his voice low. "Look, I've told you that mine is worth a fortune. The sample tested the highest I've ever seen in this area. You saw the vein. It's immense. Whoever owns that mine is a millionaire overnight. Yet it belongs to a murderer, a man who killed his partner over it."

There was silence for a long moment while Strome digested Flick's words. Flick waited, sitting back.

Strome made no effort to hide the puzzled look on his face. "What are you getting at?"

"We know nothing about this Garand fellow, whether he's alone in the world, whether he has a family. If he's hanged, his possessions, including the mine, would go to his next of kin if he has any."

"But wait a minute. Didn't you say you hadn't registered his claim yet? That's why we rode out there in the first place, to verify it."

Flick nodded. "That's right. He really doesn't own it until I register it. So, if I don't register it, and he's hanged, the claim is up for grabs, anybody's grabs… ours, for instance."

Strome eyed his companion suspiciously. His brows knitted. "Are you—" He shook his head. "That sounds… that don't sound very—"

"Ethical?" Flick smiled mischievously. "Maybe not, but it would be perfectly legal if we handle it right. I didn't think you were that straight-laced."

Strome took a second to process this. He was being asked to participate in something shady, if not illegal. Was he that ethical? Not really. Was he skittish of being caught? Yeah. The badge he wore didn't mean that much to him, but it was a living that saved him from hard labor to survive. He hesitated to jeopardize it for a prospect that could collapse on top of him. But, still, it sounded like Flick had it all figured out. He was curious to hear more. "No, I… no."

"Didn't think so. Look, we've got a real opportunity here, dropped right in our laps. Are we going to let it slip by?"

Strome shook his head. "Well, it sounds real tempting, but, if he doesn't hang, if somehow he gets off, he can make a lot of trouble for us. Maybe go to court and sue for the mine."

"Yes, and he might just win at that. Then where would we be?"

Strome nodded slowly. "Out of luck, I'd say."

"So we need to make our own luck here, make sure he hangs. Then, when everything quiets down, we register the claim as equal partners and reap the benefits."

Receptive, Strome listened closely as Flick continued. "You and I are the only ones who heard him confess. We can both testify that he admitted to killing that old man to cut him out of the claim, that he planned the whole thing. Then his story about the old man trying to kill him, about it being self-defense, won't hold up. If we both tell the same story, two against one, we can guarantee he'll hang."

Strome grinned. "Yeah, we might just be able to pull that off."

Flick matched the grin. "As long as we're careful, I'm sure we can." They both drank up.

GARAND WATCHED THE DOOR LEADING into the cell block for the arrival of the jailer. It was time for the noon meal on the third day of his incarceration, and he awaited the man who would bring it. He had now settled down to calmly thinking about what he could do to extricate himself. Having already struck up a bit of a relationship with the slow-witted jailer named Stretch, he noted the pattern of the man's comings and goings. From the man's actions and reactions, he surmised Stretch could probably be easily fooled.

The cell block door opened. Seconds later, the tall, scrawny man with the almost bald head stepped in carrying a cloth-draped tray of food. Stretch's clothes were a bit ragged and in need of laundering. He carried a percussion revolver high on his hip in a worn military type holster. His long, big-nosed face was gaunt and had a grayish pallor to it, suggesting he was not in the best of health. His breathing was labored, and he had an incessant grin that seemed eerie. "Got your dinner here." His voice was high pitched and had a Southern twang to it. He approached the cell.

Garand watched Stretch carefully, recalling the man's seemingly rehearsed movements from previous trips. He would come to the cell door, place the tray on the floor, cross to the wall to get the key, unlock and open the door, then stoop to pick up the tray. This pattern presented several opportunities for Garand to overpower the man and achieve his escape.

Stretch went through his movements, opening the cell door wide enough to fit the tray through. Garand waited until his back was turned and he bent over to pick up the tray. He stepped in and wrapped an arm around Stretch's neck, forcing pressure against the throat area. Lifting the taller man, Garand straightened up, arching his back and forcing Stretch back. Stretch's height made it difficult for Garand to take him off his feet, but he bent back as far as he could, immobilizing the man. Garand hauled in a deep breath and exerted pressure on Stretch's windpipe, holding that position while Stretch flailed his arms uselessly and gurgled as his air intake was cut. Garand's brute strength and the element of surprise worked in his favor. Grunting, he held on tightly. Stretch struggled, furiously at first, then less strenuously. After what seemed to Garand like minutes, Stretch's defenses crumbled as he slipped first into reluctant submission, then into unconsciousness.

Convinced Stretch was no longer a threat, Garand relaxed his grip and let the man slump to the floor beside the food tray. Taking a second to settle himself, Garand quickly reached for the revolver, fumbling with the holster flap and finally pulling the gun free. This he jammed into his waistband.

He had to move now. There was no telling how long Stretch would be out or when the deputy might show up. It was now or maybe never. He stepped over Stretch and made for the door, carefully opening it to survey the office section before entering. A quick look around assured him no one was there. Moving briskly, he crossed to the street door and stopped. He couldn't just barge out into the street without first checking. Opening the door enough for a look, he saw a clear path to the other side of the street. There an idle saddle horse stood at a hitch rail. A stroke of luck. He burst onto the boardwalk and ran across the dirt street to the hitch rail. In one motion, he released the horse's reins and swung into the saddle. Instantly, he was at a gallop, racing up the street, heading toward the nearby mountains.

7

IN THE SACRISTY IN THE rear of the mission church, which also served as the *padre's* living quarters, the meal was of simple Mexican fare, *tortillas,* chunked chicken, rice, and various condiments. *Padre* Cortez sat at the head of the small wooden table with Lon and Rhiann seated on either side. He poured wine made from the mission's vineyard and clasped his hands to say grace. His guests bowed their heads and folded their hands.

"Dear Lord, thank you for these fine gifts and for protecting your people with your Grace. And thank you for bringing Alonzo and Rhiann safely to our midst. Bless them and their coming union. May it be happy and fruitful."

Lon glanced at Rhiann with an expectant smile. She smiled back, wondering if, one day, she would bear his child. She saw that as a long-term prospect, since there was still much to accomplish, even in her new role as Mrs. Pearce, before settling down to raise a child. As well, what was Lon's attitude toward children? A subject they'd never touched on, she resolved to broach it at a more opportune time.

The *padre* made the sign of the cross. "God bless you both."

"Amen," they said in unison.

As they ate, *Padre* Cortez guided the conversation to learn what transpired during their adventure in New Mexico.

Lon shrugged. "Reckon I done what the governor asked, and he was mighty grateful."

Rhiann qualified the statement. "Lon is being modest, *Padre*. He earned his amnesty almost at the cost of his life."

"You weren't injured, I hope."

"Just a mite banged up, nothing serious."

The *padre* beamed. "The Lord watched over you, I'm sure. And now you're free of your past. What are your plans for the future your amnesty allows you?"

Lon chuckled. "Funny, Rhiann asked me the same thing. Reckon we decided to head to Oregon. New country up there. I'm a pretty fair cowhand. Figure to get a job punching cows, save up for some land, and start up a little spread."

"And, while Lon is doing that, I plan to open a private detective agency and put my experience to use."

The *padre* beamed at them and clapped his hands together. "This makes me very happy, to know you have definite plans and the opportunity to realize them. Truly, God is good."

"Say, you ain't going to get in trouble with the Church marrying us, are you?"

Lon's question turned the priest serious. "No, Alonzo, I will not. One of the reasons the Church has seen fit to place me here in this remote location is that, back in New York, I was looked upon as a bit of a trouble maker, a radical. The powers that be thought it prudent to send me where my actions and my nontraditional beliefs wouldn't make them... uncomfortable. Canon law does forbid a priest from marrying non-Catholics unless they convert. But, here in this remote village, I am not only these people's spiritual leader, but I am also the equivalent of, what you call in the States, a justice of the peace. So, my friends, I have the authority to marry you under the civil laws of Mexico. It will be legal, and the Church will not be officially involved. And I doubt the American authorities will question its validity."

Lon looked at the *padre* knowingly and smiled. "Always figured you for some kinda maverick, *Padre*. Now I know it's true."

Padre Cortez smiled back. "God always finds a way. Our way will be a simple ceremony here in the sacristy where you will exchange vows in your own words."

Rhiann beamed. "I was never partial to big weddings. This is more to my liking."

Lon nodded. "Works for me too."

A FEW MINUTES AFTER THE meal was finished, Rhiann stood facing Lon with *Padre* Cortez to their sides. Lon held her hands in his and listened carefully to her words. "A few months ago, I went in search of an outlaw and found more in that one meeting than I knew I was looking for. I found you, and I also found, with every passing day, I loved you more than when I first saw you. I'm happy, Lon." Her voice cracked with emotion. "And I can't wait to be your wife." Tears of joy formed in her dark eyes, welling up to stream down her cheeks.

Lon looked deeply into her liquid eyes and smiled. Instinctively, he reached his hand to her cheek to brush away the tears, then resumed holding her hands in his. He had to clear his throat. "I reckon the same goes for me. I been running just about half my life, afraid to let anyone in 'cause running ain't no life to put on no one." He cleared his throat again. "You showed me it's possible. You showed me the way to get 'er done legal-like, how to get my life back. You accepted me when no one else would, 'cepting the *padre* here and the folks at the mission. I love you more'n I ever thought it's possible to love anyone, and I want to spend the rest of my life with you."

The *padre* placed his hand on theirs. "I know this will be a good marriage between two people who are committed to each other. I remind you that marriage is until death and is not to be taken lightly.

The journey you embark on now must be as one. Decisions must be made as one. Your lives must be lived as one. Care for each other as you would care for yourselves." He made the sign of the cross, blessing them and their union. "By the authority vested in me by the government of Mexico and the laws of this province, I pronounce that you are husband and wife. I wish you every happiness."

Rhiann stood there for a long moment, savoring this time. She stared into Lon's eyes through joyful tears, and he did the same. Then, as if on cue, they came together in a loving kiss to seal the bargain.

Padre Cortez stood back and applauded them.

When they leaned back a few seconds later, ending the kiss, they were grinning wider than seemed possible.

The *padre* clapped his hands together once more. "Congratulations, my friends. Please enjoy more wine in celebration. I'll see to your room so you can spend your first night comfortably together as Mister and Missus Pearce." He took his leave quickly as they kissed again.

THE ACCOMMODATIONS THE *PADRE* SHOWED them to were as rudimentary as the rest of the mission. A standalone adobe cottage with a red half-circle tile roof in a secluded portion of the complex, it consisted of a single large room and was furnished with rustic type furniture the functionality of which far outweighed its aesthetic attraction. It was decorated in the Catholic tradition, with religious paintings and statues. *Padre* Cortez explained this was kept for visiting church dignitaries, the likes of whom almost never came to places as out of the way as St. Mary's. He opened the door and stepped aside to allow them admittance.

Rhiann looked around the room. *"Padre,* this is lovely."

Lon echoed her sentiment. "Surely is."

The *padre* stood in the doorway, his hand on the doorknob. "I'm glad you like it. It's yours for as long as you wish to stay with us." He pulled the door closed.

Rhiann sauntered around the room observing the appointments but found herself gravitating toward the bed, the plain wood frame with the irregular outlines of the mattress covered by a colorful blanket of local origins. She stopped there.

"I'd be lying if I said this piece of furniture didn't attract me the most of anything in this room."

Lon moved close behind her. His arms snaked around her waist and drew her back to him. "I'd be lying if I said I didn't agree with you."

She turned within his grasp, bringing her face close to his and kissed him, a long, inviting, seductive kiss. It was all right now. They were married. They were legal. They had permission to do everything they'd waited until now to even think about.

When the kiss ended, Lon smiled sheepishly. "I ain't promising much in the way of knowhow. Likely, I'll be all thumbs, but, if you'll bear with me, I reckon 'twixt the two of us, we'll cipher it out."

She grinned as she whispered, "I'm sure we will."

And they did. Over the next few hours, they explored each other both physically and emotionally in ways each had only dreamed of.

Wrapped in each other's arms, Lon whispered in her ear, "I didn't hurt you, did I?"

Rhiann, taken with how gentle and caring he was and how he'd tried to do everything right, drew him closer to her. "No, Lon, you didn't hurt me. Of course not."

"I don't ever want to hurt you."

"I know that, but you don't have to treat me like some delicate flower either. I don't break that easily."

"Well, in that case…." He nuzzled her neck, prompting her to let out a giggle.

Finally, spent and exhausted, they slept together as lovers for the first time.

THEY DIDN'T VENTURE OUTSIDE UNTIL close to noon the next day. Greeted by people who'd been acquainted with Lon during his first stay at the mission, Lon took the opportunity to introduce Rhiann to them as his wife. She regarded the pride he exuded in doing so. She also noted the respect the people had for him and imagined the many ways he must have helped them when he lived among them. This added to the love and respect she had for him.

After visiting with the residents, they had lunch with *Padre* Cortez in the sacristy. The conversation centered on Rhiann's plan to open a detective agency and the *padre's* fascination with that concept.

"It boggles my imagination, a woman in charge of a detective agency in what I understand to be largely a man's domain in a lawless wilderness. You would be putting yourself in a dangerous situation."

"No more dangerous than being a Pinkerton agent. And why not put my training to use in a territory that obviously lacks law and order? I'd rather do that than have to spend the time learning something new."

Lon leaned in. "Not like she'd be going this alone. I'll be right there to help if need be."

The *padre* nodded. "I can see you've given this a good amount of thought. I wish you well in your new endeavors."

Later, while Rhiann learned some cooking secrets from the women, Lon chopped wood and gave a hand where he could, then cared for Gray and their other animals. After spending another night at the cottage, they rose early and prepared to leave for the long journey to Oregon. At the conclusion of breakfast, they left the sacristy with *Padre* Cortez and approached the already saddled horses and the packed mule.

The *padre* blessed them and their animals. "I pray you will always be happy and that you will achieve your goals. I realize it's a long journey, but you will always be welcome here. If you can, sometime in the future, please come visit an old man."

Lon shook his hand. "No idea what the future holds, but if we can, we will. Thanks for everything, *Padre.* You take care."

"And you as well. You will always be in my prayers."

They mounted and rode toward the great door as the old man swung it open. Waving, they rode through the opening and into the vast Mexican plain, heading northwest.

GARAND RODE THE STOLEN HORSE hard into the foothills west of Colinas de Oro, trying to put as much distance between himself and the law as possible before the animal began to tire. He had no food, no water, a loaded revolver with no additional ammunition, and a horse with which he was unfamiliar. His prospects for survival in the mountains were almost nil, unless he adapted to his surroundings. With no choice in the matter, he vowed he would.

He directed the horse into rougher country as glances behind him showed the town becoming a smaller picture on the eastern horizon. Climbing steep hills into higher altitudes quickly tired and winded the animal. Garand was forced to pull up to give the horse a breather. Midday heat radiated down on them. He removed his hat and wiped sweat from his face with his grimy sleeve. The need to reach a safe hiding place before nightfall became his primary goal. To accomplish that, he needed the horse. He could not afford to allow it to falter. Water had to be found quickly before they went on. He relaxed his hold on the reins to let the horse go its own way to sniff out water. After a few minutes for a blow, the horse began moving again, without Garand's direction.

Ten minutes into the ride bore fruit. Through a stand of pines, a stream of clear flowing water became visible. The horse moved quickly straight to it, rushed in up to its fetlocks, and sucked in the clean liquid. Garand dismounted and crouched beside the horse, allowing the water to seep into his trousers and shoes, while he cupped handfuls to drink and splash in his face. Silently, he thanked the animal for seeking out the stream.

Refreshed, Garand surveyed the area around the brook. This was fresh water, probably fed by runoffs of melting snow from high in the mountains. A pine forest surrounded the stream, providing shade from the sun. He was still too close to the town for comfort, but if he followed the water's course, going against the current, he might find a spot just as inviting far enough away to avoid the deputy and a posse who would surely come searching for him. He stood up and mounted, now with a plan in mind. The tributary seemed to run from the northwest. Turning the horse in that direction, he continued, staying in the water to avoid leaving a trail. His progress would be slower but safer.

Winding into the mountains, the brook narrowed after a few miles, moving from the forest into an open area and into another stand of pines. Garand stayed with it until a glance at the sun told him it was late afternoon, time for him to seek out a suitable campsite and put up for the night. He directed the horse onto dry land and entered the trees. It was cooler at this altitude and promised to be a chilly evening, if not downright cold. Quickly, he sought out a clearing that would accommodate a fire without the possibility of setting the entire forest ablaze. Overhead clearance was essential. He knew that much about camping but not much more.

Dismounting, he took time to check the contents of the saddle bags. He found a set of hobbles which would keep the horse from wandering off, as well as a pack of beef jerky, some matches, and a box of .44 caliber cartridges, totally useless for loading the percussion revolver he'd taken from the jailer.

After securing the hobbles to the horse's front legs as the animal grazed, he gnawed off several bites of the jerky and foraged for small broken branches to use as kindling to start a fire. He placed it in the center of the clearing and went into the trees to find hefty fallen branches small enough to add to the blaze. This would keep the camp warm through the night. A match got it going. He rolled out the blanket tied behind the saddle, hoping it would be enough to retain his body heat while he slept.

Through the darkness he dozed a bit and thought a lot, deciding to move on to the mine the next day. Realizing that might be the first place a posse would look for him, he concocted an elaborate plan to turn the mine location into a secure facility that would protect him while he worked the claim. He would need men he could trust who would guard him and work for him for the promise of shares in the profits. To accomplish this, he would need funds, the gold he'd buried at the mine site a few weeks earlier. That would do it. He'd sneak in and unearth it. Then, he'd head north to the nearby Oregon Territory. Surely there he'd find willing participants. Satisfied with his strategy, he rolled over and slept soundly.

A FEW DAYS INTO HIS flight from Colinas de Oro, Garand adapted quickly to his new surroundings. He devised traps by covering small holes in the ground with brush and luring scavenging animals with bits of jerky. Through trial and error, he learned to kill the trapped animals, then skin and gut them using a hunting knife he'd found in a saddle bag. He used branches from around the campsite to impale and roast his kills. He employed the skin of one of the animals as a water bladder and tied it off with a rawhide thong cut from the saddle. When he left the camp after a week, he was satisfied at being self-sufficient enough to survive in the wilderness.

Depending on his developing sense of direction, he found his way southeast to the general location of the mine, staying to unused paths and underbrush. As he entered the area, the lay of the land became familiar. Approaching from behind the mine location, he dismounted and tied the horse off on a stout branch. Uncertain if the site was deserted, he moved in as quietly as possible from the north side, crouching in bushes, descending the grade behind the cabin. As he reached level ground, directly behind the spot he'd buried Hirsch's body, movement became evident in the work area. Sounds of voices reached him. He crept to the rear of the cabin and moved carefully along its side for a better view of who or what had invaded the area.

Emerging from the mineshaft, three familiar figures entered the open area. Strome, the deputy, led the way. Flick, the assayer, followed closely. And the jailer, Stretch, came last, wandering a bit. Garand crouched to stay hidden. He watched and listened.

Strome turned back to address Flick. "I got to get back to town and keep up appearances. Folks are looking to me to lead the posse out again, so I got to go do that."

"All right, we'll keep working here. Bring out some supplies when you get chance, and bring more help."

"Right." Strome left them and walked to the corral where their horses were tied. He mounted and left the compound.

The knowledge fell on Garand like a load of bricks. *Son of a bitch!* They'd jumped the claim. He was a fugitive, and they moved right in. Maybe, if he hadn't escaped, they'd planned to railroad him into a hangman's noose. Now they were bringing more people into this, most likely from that town. Were they all corrupt there? Did it matter to no one that this claim was his, that he'd merely defended himself when Hirsch had attacked him, that he deserved better than being hanged and tossed to the side? No. This would not stand. He would take back what was his and make these interlopers pay for their transgressions. Now, certainly, he needed men to aid him, men who cared not what was legal but what was lucrative, to punish those who stood against him.

Garand moved to the relative safety of the rear of the cabin as Flick and Stretch started toward the front. When he was certain he was out of their sight, he climbed a few feet of the hill and stopped at an odd shaped bush. He dropped to one knee and clawed at the earth to reveal a leather sack with a rawhide tie holding it closed. A nod acknowledging the success of the dig put him on his way to the top of the hill, concealed by bushes and taller grass. He retrieved the horse, mounted, and struck out northwest toward the California/Oregon border.

8

COVERING TWENTY MILES A DAY for a week landed Garand inside the Oregon line. The first established settlement he came upon after crossing the border was no bigger than Colinas de Oro and considerably more ramshackle. Populated in large part by trappers, hunters, and hangers-on of questionable repute, it consisted of a few commercial buildings, several saloons and supply houses, and very few residences. As he approached, a rudimentary sign marker on the side of the trail announced the location, *Hadley, Ore. pop. 208.* The population numbers had been stricken through several times with no attempt at neatness.

The single dirt street was home to randomly placed buildings. Each appeared to have sprung up on its own with no planning to fit in with the others. Garand rode slowly, wearily, taking in the crude identifying signs on the out-of-square false fronts. *General Mercantile* on one. *Liquor & Eats* on another. Barely legible, they just about served their purposes.

Thirst attracted the horse to a water trough in front of a saloon. Garand allowed the animal its will, winding up in front of the place marked *Liquor & Eats.* As the horse drank its fill, Garand dismounted, surveying this crude attempt at a village. Two things crossed his mind. First, based on the few people he'd observed so far on the street, he would definitely find here the cut of men he sought. He'd scour the place for the best candidates. The second thought he had was his need to clean himself up. He'd seen no hotel here, so a room and a bed were out of the question. Could he at least locate some new clothes? He had money now, having exchanged some of the gold he'd taken from the mine into cash along the way. The general store should have something in his size. Tugging at the horse's reins, he led the animal across the street to the store, tied it off, and entered.

Fifteen minutes later, he emerged wearing a fresh outfit. Somewhat renewed, he led the horse across to the saloon, tied it to the building's hitch rail, and took a walk to look the town over. Checking carefully as he walked, he saw no one who would fill the bill as his enforcers. He returned to the *Liquor & Eats* place. Muffled voices and laughter came from inside, indicating at least several occupants who seemed to be enjoying themselves.

He entered through the batwings, pausing there to survey the interior. It was a simple affair, a large room with a makeshift bar running along the rear wall. The bar itself was made up of standing empty beer barrels and a single wooden plank. Uneven, at that. It came to no higher than an average man's thigh. Behind it, a pudgy man with slicked down hair and a handlebar mustache toyed with a dingy bar rag. He seemed cut from the same mold as the cloth. Beyond the barkeep, in crates turned sideways, liquor bottles rested one on the other. A tapped beer keg supported by an upright hogshead stood ready to dispense. The beer would be room temperature, since the town appeared too small and too remote to offer amenities like an ice house.

The conversations and laughter continued on both sides of him as he approached the bar.

"What'll it be?" The bartender's voice was a deep growl as Garand reached the bar.

"Beer, please." He was not fond of warm beer, but, in need of a clear head, he'd avoid the hard stuff.

The barman stooped and reached into one of two basins at his feet. It held a liquid that appeared to be soapy water. He extracted a glass and dipped it several times into a neighboring tub that contained a semblance of clear water. Rising, he shook off the excess droplets, filled the glass from the keg, and set the thing, mostly foam, in front of Garand. "Two bits."

Garand fished the coin from his pocket and dropped it on the plank before lifting the beer. After a healthy swig, he wiped foam from his whiskered upper lip and looked around at those occupying the place, scrutinizing each face. Which ones would be his candidates?

He ignored the talk, largely unintelligible anyway, but he scrutinized the men from whom the noise came. There were about ten of them, and they were filthier than he, if that was even possible. Their body odors, combined with the smell of cheap liquor, stale beer, and tobacco smoke and juice, became instantly offensive to him. These men were dressed in some form of work clothes, be it lumberjack, trapper, or even cowhand, but yet none seemed to be gainfully employed, else why would they be grouped here in midday? He was sure he would find those he sought among them.

He settled on a group of eight men seated together on benches at a long rough-hewn table. They appeared to be sturdy enough to handle themselves in a fight. One of them stood out.

Short and stocky, the man sat sprawled on the bench, an elbow on the table and his legs extended. His round face carried a constant scowl and had at least a week's growth of beard as well. Squinty eyes under a floppy hat gave him an ominous appearance. The Colt holstered on his hip accentuated the image. He watched Garand's approach carefully. "Hell you looking at?" His voice had a sneer to it.

Garand stopped in front of him. "You. I'm interested in you."

"That supposed to mean something to me?"

Garand detected belligerence and sought to head it off. He raised his hand in a halting gesture. "No, no. I don't want any trouble or to cause any. I mean to hire some men to help me. I thought you and your friends might be interested."

The man shrugged. "Can't say till I hear the whole of it."

Garand moved closer and gestured to the seat next to the man. "May I?"

The man shrugged. "Suit yourself."

"My name is Victor Garand. What's yours?"

"I still ain't heard nothing tells me what you're up to. Till I do, I ain't saying no more."

Garand continued. "I own a gold mine in California."

"Well, ain't that just peachy." His mocking manner changed to impatience. "Looky here, mister whatever-your-name-is, you tell me something good or get the hell away from me."

"All right, look, my claim was jumped, and I'm seeking help in getting it back."

"Sounds like work for the law. I sure ain't no lawman. What do you want with me?"

"The law had a hand in screwing me over. They framed me for murder and jailed me so I couldn't register the claim. Then they ripped it out from under me, the assayer and the deputy both. I need some men who aren't particular about how they do things to help me take it back from them."

He looked Garand up and down, now showing interest. "What's in it for me and the boys?"

"I'll cut you in for equal shares."

"Shares of what? How much we talking here?"

"I hit a mother lode. It assayed out higher than anything they've ever seen." Garand set his beer glass on the table. He pulled the sack from inside his shirt, opened it and took out a nugget. This he placed in the man's hand.

A quick examination brought an interested expression. "Looks pure enough. Can't tell what it's worth, but it ain't chunk change."

"It's pure all right, and there's plenty more there, no telling how much. Interested?"

The man nodded.

Garand held out the open sack for the sample to be dropped back in. "Are you ready to tell me your name now?"

"Rawls."

"How do you do, Mister Rawls. I'd like you and your friends to ride back to the claim with me and take control of it, by force if necessary."

Their faces glazed over, telling Garand his speech might sound "high and mighty" to them.

Rawls was thoughtful. "Hmm. You talk funny-like." He took a beat, studying Garand. "I'll talk it over with the boys. You know how it is. We all get a say."

"I understand. I'll wait outside if you like."

Rawls nodded. "That'll work."

Garand got up and walked through the swinging doors, waiting in the shade on the side of the building, uncertain how this would go. One thought occurred to him, giving him cause for alarm. What if they turned on him? What would he do against the superior odds they presented? He put it aside to wait.

Discussion inside went on for several minutes. Only muffled voices could be heard. When they stopped, Garand stepped around to the batwings as Rawls came through them.

"We'll go along with you, but you got to outfit us, and no skimping."

"I will, but I'm concerned about one thing."

"Yeah? What's that?"

"It occurred to me that you could just string me along until you get me alone on the trail and then kill me and take my gold."

Rawls flashed a look that could kill. "You calling me a liar?"

Garand's hands came up in that halting gesture again. "No, no, it's just a concern, that's all."

"Yeah, sure, we could do that. Easy enough. Ain't even got to get you alone. We could do it right here, right now. Nobody in this place cares about nobody. But ain't nothing smart about that. You weigh one poke a nuggets agin what you say's in the mine, taking you now don't make good sense. Sides, we don't even know where your claim is. Turns out you're lying or things ain't what you say they is, we can always do you in, no problem. We got the numbers." Rawls shook his head. "Naw, we'll play this out, see what happens."

Only slightly reassured, Garand accepted the fact that trust would need to be gained on both sides. He nodded slowly as he considered the situation. "I guess we have a deal."

A GUARDED ALLIANCE FORMED BETWEEN Garand and the bunch headed by Rawls. Garand provided the funds to properly outfit the group for the trip back to California. Rawls and his men readily accepted the deal and its projected proceeds, dictating to Garand those items that would add comfort and convenience to the journey. A day later, with the addition of two fully laden pack horses, they rode out of Hadley, heading south.

Their stops were enhanced with tasty trail food and the products of short hunting jaunts. Their nights were passed in tents and cozy sleeping bags. The abundance of supplies negated the need for stopping at towns along the way, allaying the concerns of several of the men who were wanted by the law in California. They arrived in the vicinity of the mine a week later, none the worse for wear. Arising early from their last night of travel, Garand held a meeting as they ate their morning meal.

"The mine is just over those hills back there." He pointed over his shoulder as Rawls, and the others listened intently. "If we bull our way in there without some kind of a plan, we may be in over our heads. There's no telling how many we'll be up against. Rawls, I think you and I should go in alone. That way you can see the layout and figure out what will work."

The men nodded agreement. After breakfast, Garand and Rawls left the camp, riding for the mine. Cresting the north hill bordering the canyon, they dismounted and tied off in the bushes a safe distance away. Garand led the way to a vantage point with a full view of the area. As they crouched behind some brush, Garand, speaking low, described the layout. Rawls took it all in, remarking that he'd counted five men working outside the shaft, but he had no idea how many were inside. Garand brought up the possibility that others might be inside the cabin.

Rawls gave it some thought. "This ain't going to be no pushover, but if we can get a good count a how many they got, we can figure something out to catch 'em off guard and nail 'em 'fore they know what hit 'em. Let's hang here a mite and count heads."

Garand was impressed with Rawls's initiative. He'd obviously done this sort of thing before. "Sure, we've got plenty of time."

During their hour-long observance, Garand pointed out Flick, Strome, and Stretch. There were others he'd seen in passing in the town, but he didn't know their names or anything about them. Suffice to say they were complicit in the plans to work the stolen mine and were probably aware, if not suspicious, of the circumstances leading up to the acquisition. Their presence indicated their indifference, making them just as guilty in Garand's eyes. They would be included, with the three he knew, in his plans to retake and work the claim.

At the end of their reconnoiter, Rawls drew back from the bush they used as concealment. "I seen enough. Time to go figure this out."

Back at camp, another meeting was held.

"It's a good setup for an ambush." With a stick, Rawls sketched out a rough drawing of the landscape in the dirt as he spoke. "It's boxed in on three sides. Hills on the sides and a rock wall in the back. One road in. Plenty of cover on the hills. We got enough men to set three on each hill and two on the trail leading in. We cut loose from the hills and any of 'em gets away gets picked off by the two on the trail."

Garand studied the plan. "That's not how I want this to go."

Rawls glanced up from the outline. "Yeah? How's that?"

"I want them taken alive."

Rawls's expression turned to complete confusion. "Alive? You loco? What the hell're we supposed to do with them alive?"

"Unless you men like the idea of laboring as miners, they can be forced to do the actual work in the mine. All you've got to do is guard them."

Rawls paused in thought. "Hmm. You might got something there. Might could work. What do you boys think?"

Garand became intense, interrupting their attempt at discussion. "Oh, I know it'll work. I thought a lot about this. Those bastards owe me, not only for jumping my claim, but for making a fugitive out of me. And the ones who've joined them are just as complicit. Killing's too easy for them. Alive, we get free labor out of them, and all we have to do is sit on them, make them do the work, and count the profits."

Rawls had a question. "What about where they come from? They disappear, ain't nobody coming looking for 'em?"

"From what I've seen of the citizens of Colinas de Oro, they couldn't care less what happens."

A few of the men offered approving words. One said he'd rather not work. Another agreed it was easier to push others than to do it himself.

Rawls nodded. "Yeah, I like that. Like having our own chain gang."

Garand flashed a grin. "Exactly. If and when the mine plays out, that'll be time enough to get rid of them. And we can go live like kings."

Several cheers went up at those words. Then Rawls took a serious note. "Check your irons and your shells. The way I got this planned, everything gots to work like clockwork. No slip-ups."

9

RAWLS WORKED HIS STRATEGY, PLACING his men. In a group circled around him at a point a short distance from the mine site, he issued his orders. "Paco, Snake, Hatcher, I want you on the north slope. Spread out and find cover." Paco, the stubby Mexican with the rotten teeth, Snake, the skinny, lanky whip-wielder, and Hatcher, the hulking ex-buffalo hunter with the Sharps fifty caliber, nodded. "Foley, Red, and Lakota, you circle around to the south ridge. Get you good cover and spread out like these three." Foley, the cowboy Rawls had met in prison and formed a bond with, Red, the lumberjack, and Lakota, the only name the aging Sioux medicine man answered to, indicated their agreement. Except for Hatcher and his Sharps, each was armed with a pistol caliber long gun. The last man, Drawden, the ex-Army sharpshooter, had already been placed with Garand. They now rode in a wide circle to avoid alerting the occupants as they reached the entrance road into the mine. "Pick you a good spot so's you can pick off any strays when the fireworks start." From his high vantage point, Rawls watched them skirting the hills toward their locations.

Satisfied with the plan, he reviewed it as he made his way across the craggy top rocks that formed the back wall framing the mine complex to take his place as the fourth man on the north hill, above the cabin. He crouched behind bushes and waited as activities at the mine went on without suspicion.

AT THE ENTRANCE ROAD, GARAND and Drawden drew rein after descending a slight rise on the north slope. Drawden dismounted and, ground tying his mount, found a suitable boulder, reaching to his hips, to use as concealment. He crouched and shouldered his rifle, prepared to sight in on whomever came his way.

Remaining mounted, Garand observed the activity in and around the mine operation, concentrating on trying to pick out those he most wanted to confront. However, neither Flick nor Strome were in view. He waited, continuing to scrutinize.

As minutes ticked by, his mind wandered, back to when he was a teacher, when he adhered to ethics, when he tried to impart righteous beliefs to those in his charge. Where did that go? And when? Was it when he left his work and his life back east? Was it after he observed the baser human activities prevalent in the gold camps? No, it was when he first met Hirsch and the possibility of actually becoming rich was held out to him. The turning point was the attack, the unfounded attack by a gold-crazed Hirsch, and his own horrible reaction to it. The more he considered it, the more he came to the realization that killing Hirsch was no accident. His desire for *all* the gold, not just an equal share, motivated his overzealous defense. Every decision, every move he'd made after that was with that intention in mind. Not so he noticed at the time, but, in retrospect, there could be no other reason.

Now he was about to set a plan in motion that would enslave those responsible for his current situation, and he had no qualms about any of it. In reality, he looked forward to it. Revenge would be his, and it would be sweet. He would revel in it, and he would benefit from the labors it produced. Nothing and no one would stand in his way.

His reverie was interrupted after an unknown amount of time had passed as Drawden called to him.

"You going to move or what?"

Without answering, Garand touched his heels to his horse's flanks and began a slow walk up the road, unconcerned he was in plain sight of the workers. He rode bigger than life straight into the operation as if he belonged there. On the periphery, a few men working the refining machinery outside the shaft noticed his arrival. One of them hot-footed it into the cabin and seconds later emerged with Flick. Just the man Garand wanted to see.

Stopping in the center of the yard, the assayer, hands on his hips, gawked at Garand for a few seconds in disbelief and then shouted over his shoulder. "Strome, get out here!"

The deputy hurried from inside the shaft and stopped dead just outside the opening when he got a look at Garand. He jerked the sidearm out of its holster and leveled the weapon on Garand as he approached slowly. "You get down from there, down on your knees, hands behind your head."

Garand stayed put. "You're not the one giving the orders here, I am." He said it loudly and emphatically enough to be heard by every-one in the camp.

Strome continued closing on Garand. Flick fell in behind him and stopped when he did, about ten feet from Garand's horse. "What the hell you talking about, you are? You're goddamn surrounded."

"We'll see about that." Garand stood in his stirrups. "Rawls!"

At the call, Rawls raised his rifle and placed a shot inches from the deputy's feet. The crack echoed off the hills and faded. "More where that come from, gents." He levered another round in place, loud enough to be heard. "They's a bead drawed on everyone a you. Drop your guns and get your hands where we can see 'em. Make a move and we'll cut you down."

From the opposite hill, Hatcher fired the Sharps into the ground near a bunch of shuffling feet. Louder than Rawls's Winchester, the sound bounced off the walls even longer. People backed away, glancing around in all directions, acknowledging Garand's upper hand.

Hesitation, apprehension, and downright fear all converged in the next few seconds as the captives bunched together. Flick and Strome stood transfixed in their spots, Strome's revolver poised, still aimed at Garand.

Rawls's sharp voice cut the silence. "Drop 'em."

As Garand dismounted, guns hit the dirt quickly. He walked with determination to Strome and ripped the gun from his hand. Staring intensely for a second, Garand swatted the deputy across the face with an open hand, sending him back a few feet, colliding with Flick. Flick stumbled. Both men managed to remain standing.

Now armed with a more modern revolver than the percussion model he'd taken from the jailer, Garand aimed the weapon at both men, an angry scowl on his face. "Rawls, bring the men in." He took a step toward Flick, causing the assayer to back up. "This is all your doing, you son of a bitch. You engineered this from the start. Now you'll suffer the consequences."

At Garand's order, each of Rawls's men stood up, his rifle leveled on the group. The sight of them convinced the workers to raise their hands in surrender. The intruders made their way down the slopes, never taking their eyes or their weapons off their subjects. They moved in to cover them. Drawden was the last to join them, riding in carrying his sniper rifle.

Rawls stopped beside Garand and gave Flick and Strome the once-over. "Them the ones you talked about?"

"They are."

"Don't look so smart now, do they?" Rawls watched them cower.

"No, they don't. Now we'll find out how hard they can work." Garand turned toward the rest of the captives. "That goes for the rest of you as well. This mine belongs to me and now so do you."

IN SHORT ORDER, THE PRISONERS' discarded weapons were collected and stowed in the cabin while they were herded together under heavy guard with Rawls's men surrounding them. Fear was evident in their faces as their eyes darted around, desperately searching for an escape that was not to come.

Outside the cabin, Garand conferred alone with Rawls. "I don't want to lose a minute getting that ore out, but we need to take some time to get things organized. I foresee this as a long-term operation, so I think the first order of business should be to build a shelter for you and your men, as well as a place where Paco can cook."

"Red knows a mite about building. He can run that."

Garand nodded. "Good. Tell him to take as many men as he needs and work 'em hard. In the meantime, you men can use the tents."

"Where you figure them others can sleep?"

"For all I care, the ground's good enough for them. We'll need a schedule to guard them around the clock."

"I'll handle that."

A day after the attack, Garand enlisted Hatcher to harness horses to the buckboard Flick had lodged at the camp. He gave Hatcher a wad of paper money.

"Colinas de Oro is about eight miles east of here. I want you to search out as much scrap metal as possible to make restraints for the prisoners. If you can't find scraps, buy what we need, and while you're at it, buy enough supplies to keep us going for a few weeks."

Rawls voiced reservations. "You sure that ain't going to make 'em ask questions?"

Garand shook his head. "Not them. As long as they're getting paid, they won't care."

Hatcher shrugged and climbed aboard the wagon, setting out on his mission.

Red quickly organized several of the prisoners into a team of carpenters and drove them relentlessly. A week later, the bunkhouse was completed. It was rudimentary but serviceable, giving Rawls and his men indoor sleeping at night while guards rotated in four-hour shifts to ensure the prisoners remained in place. From there, under Red's and Paco's supervision, a cook shack was constructed with an open-air fire pit behind it. The mine operation then resumed using guard overseen slave labor. Within a week, Garand had a regular schedule of work assignments set up. He placed the most physically fit men in the shaft to swing pickaxes that would chip out chunks of rock from the gold vein. Others would transport the ore from the shaft to the equipment to break it down and separate the gold nuggets. Still others would operate the machinery. Work was to be conducted under guard during daylight hours.

Standing outside the cabin, which he had taken over as his residence, Garand watched the activity that would ultimately make him rich and fell into deep thought. The two who had sniped him and the minions who followed them were all getting what was coming to them. And he enjoyed seeing it happen. Months before, he would have never thought himself capable of retaliation of this magnitude. But he considered that growth, learning from deeds done to him, to be freeing of mind and body. Nothing was sacred anymore, and nothing would be too far-fetched to deter him.

He focused on Flick, working at the refining equipment, and saw a slot for him. "Assayer! Come here!"

Flick responded wearily, obviously not accustomed to physical labor, and made his way toward the cabin. He said nothing when he reached Garand.

"Inside." Garand gestured toward the cabin door.

Flick complied.

Garand followed him in and closed the door. "I'm giving you the chance to get out from under physical labor. You'll assay whatever they dig out. But, if you step out of line or try to pull anything, I'll kill you outright, no second chances, and find someone else to run the assays. Do we have an understanding?"

Flick studied his captor for a moment, then he nodded. "Y-yeah, all right."

"Then get to work."

Ore was extracted from the vein quickly and, thanks to Hirsch's mechanical innovations, was processed into gold nuggets. Flick confirmed the stuff to be at the highest reading he'd ever encountered. The vein became purer the deeper they dug. Encouraged by the numbers, Garand drove the captives relentlessly, working them from dawn to dark with little water and meager food. Any who balked were dealt with harshly, most often feeling Snake's whip until they acquiesced.

A week later, Garand flexed his newly acquired "managerial skills" when he shared a thought with Rawls. "I don't know about you, but I'm getting fed up with Paco's *frijoles*. Maybe the addition of a few women who can cook would balance things. They could be useful in… other pursuits as well."

Rawls stopped to consider. "That ain't a half-bad idea. Been a spell for me. Others, too, I'm reckoning. How about we nab two or three of 'em from that town?"

"My thought exactly, but keep it on the quiet. Even though nobody seems to be aware of our presence here, and nobody there is concerned with finding the missing citizens, there's no sense inviting trouble."

"That ain't a worry. We got enough guns to take care a anybody shows up. We'll just nab 'em and add 'em to the crew."

"I understand that, but keep it under wraps just the same."

Rawls nodded. "You're the boss."

Garand looked off into the horizon. "Yes. I am."

10

Toward evening, Rawls spoke to Foley as Snake finished hitching a team to the buckboard. "Keep a close eye on things."

Foley nodded.

Rawls climbed up on the spring seat and picked up the reins. Snake sat alongside him. They started out of the yard. While Rawls drove, Snake silently gawked at the countryside and fingered the bullwhip attached in a coil to his gun belt. The timing they'd selected coordinated their arrival in Colinas de Oro with darkness, better to conceal their clandestine movements.

Rawls pulled the team up behind the buildings on the main street in a particularly unlit section. "We'll go the rest of the way on foot. Hatcher says the storekeeper's wife's a good looker. Let's start there."

"Uh-huh." Snake's reply was a smoky, low pitched grunt, seemingly unconcerned.

"What's a matter with you? I'd 'spect you to be more interested in having women around."

Snake just shrugged.

Rawls shot him a sidewise look. "Shut up. You talk too much." He looked away. The whip man didn't get it.

Their timing worked out well. Darkness blanketed the town.

Quietly, they got down and hobbled the horses' front legs, then they walked through an alley to reach the street. Except for the scheme involving the storekeeper's wife, the rest would be conducted as opportunity presented itself. They moved slowly toward the general store.

At the store's single plate-glass window, Rawls raised his hand to halt his companion, then peeked inside. He spoke in a whisper. "They're alone. Looks like they closing up. The woman just went in the back room." He stepped away from the window. "Go around back and grab her. I'll keep this joker busy long as I can."

"Yeah." Snake faded into the shadows of the alley.

Rawls entered the place, making enough noise to draw the owner's attention. He approached the small, pleasant looking young man standing behind the counter.

"Evening, sir." The high-pitched voice fit the man's size. "We're about to close, but if there's anything I can help you with...." He let that trail off.

Rawls glanced around, playing for time. "Yeah." He dragged the word out to twice its length. "I'm looking for bullets for a forty-four cap and ball pistol, not ball, mind you. I want the ones look like cones. You got any a them?"

The man took a second to digest the request, then scanned the shelves behind him where boxed ammunition was stored. "Afraid not. All I've got is ball."

Rawls shook his head. "Naw, I don't like them. Can't get 'em to seat right. You sure you ain't got none a the cone slugs?" His words came out slowly, trying to hold the clerk's attention.

"Well, everything I've got is right here." He indicated the shelves. "See? Only ball ammunition. I don't get much call for the other ones."

"Yeah, see this pistol I got, it's got a rut wore into the ramrod. It slips off'n the balls, and they don't seat hardly at all, but it grabs them cones real good, and I get a good fit. Balls don't work right." It was more information than was necessary, but it used up more time.

The owner began to show signs of frustration. "Look, sir, I sympathize with your problem, but I'm afraid I can't help you. I don't have what you're looking for. I can order it for you, but I won't have it in for at least a month or so, if you can wait that long."

Rawls feigned thought to consume more minutes.

"Sir?"

"Naw, that's okay. I'll find it somewheres else. Much obliged."

"Thank you. Come again."

Figuring he'd gone as far as he could without upsetting the storekeeper and drawing attention to himself, Rawls turned and walked out slowly. The time he'd given Snake to do the deed would have to be enough. He made his way down the alley and hurried off to where they'd left the wagon.

Snake climbed down from the wagon bed as Rawls reached it. In the darkness, he made out the form of a woman, seated in the bed. From the outline, he surmised she was bound and gagged. She squirmed around, unable to free herself, and made muffled noises, none of which were loud enough to attract the attention that might save her.

"No trouble?"

Snake shook his head. "Nope."

"Good. Let's see what else we can find."

As they emerged from the alley, an encounter in front of Taylor's Saloon piqued their interest—two women, framed by the low light coming from Taylor's engaged in an animated conversation. Rawls put his hand on Snake's arm to stop him. Silently, he motioned his head toward the disturbance. They watched.

"Why don't you just leave me alone?" The smaller of the women spoke in a frustrated tone.

"Because I want to help you," answered the taller, heavier set woman. This one was in a black dress and hat.

The smaller one waved a hand in a swatting motion. "How many times I got to tell you I don't want your help? I don't want nobody's help. I'm fine the way I am."

"But your soul is not. Rita, if you don't change your ways, your next stop could be eternal damnation. I'm trying to save you from that."

Rawls poked Snake in the ribs and started across the street.

Snake followed.

The heated exchange continued as the two men reached the women, but the women, too engrossed in each other, didn't notice them.

Rita raised her voice to a shout. "I ain't looking to be saved. Can't you get that through your thick head?"

"Listen. It's only a matter of time before you become pregnant."

"Yeah, so what if I do? There's orphanages, ain't there?"

Rawls and Snake moved in close to the women.

"Evening, ladies." Rawls spoke in a low voice. "We don't want no trouble. Just come along with us."

Rita shrank back, but the older woman stood her ground. "I beg your pardon, gentlemen, please don't interfere. This is very important."

Rawls gripped her arm, a tight hold. "So's this, lady. I ain't asking again. Come quiet or we'll make you."

Snake grabbed Rita around the waist and put a hand over her mouth. He lifted her off her feet and carted her across the street.

Rawls's grip pulled the other woman a bit off balance and toward him. "Fight me and I'll slug you one." He yanked her. "Come on." Half dragging her, he hauled her across the street, following Snake and Rita. The woman pulled at Rawls's hold and tried to get away. He stopped. "Told you." He grunted and swung his left hand in an open hand swat that snapped her head to the side. The unh she uttered was hardly audible as she sagged toward the ground. Rawls grabbed her around the waist and dragged her through the alley where Snake worked at trussing Rita up in the wagon bed.

Between the two men, they quickly tied the stunned older woman with ropes and fitted her with a gag. Snake stepped over the seat and picked up the reins as Rawls jumped down and secured the tailgate. He gathered the hobbles and tossed them under the seat, then joined Snake. "Dumb luck nobody seen that. Let's get the hell out of here."

A snap of the reins sent the wagon out of town in a hurry.

GRACE POLK OPENED HER EYES slowly to fuzzy, imperceptible images. Where… what? There was pain in the area around her cheek. It shifted her attention from determining her location to how she'd gotten here. She blinked, trying to clear her vision, while her mind raced in many directions at once. Then it started coming back to her. He'd hit her, that man who interfered with her attempt to save Rita from herself. Yes, she recalled now. He'd dragged her halfway across the street. When she pulled back to escape his grip, he turned on her and everything went black. Even that was sketchy.

What in heaven's name was this all about? Wait, what about Rita? The recollection of the other man taking Rita away drifted into her mind. Yes, they'd taken them both. But why? And where was she now, and where was Rita?

Grace shook her head to try to stabilize the swirling and clear away the cobwebs. It helped a little. The images before her became a little clearer. She was inside something, an enclosure of some kind. Very little light reached her eyes, and the lack of sharpness didn't help. She concentrated on what was in front of her. Brown. Canvas? A tent, maybe? She was in a seated position, her knees drawn up. Her ankles were tied. There was enough light to confirm that. And her arms were secured behind her. Movement drew her attention. She looked around.

Two forms, appearing to be in the same position as she, were a few feet away. Was that Rita? Possibly. Who was the other one? Not enough light or clarity to tell yet. She blinked some more, further sharpening her vision.

"Rita? Is that you?" Her voice was weak, gravelly.

"Yeah, it's me." Rita's tinny voice was unmistakable.

"W-what's going on?"

"Hell if I know. Them two bastards grabbed us and brought us here."

"Where is here?"

"I don't know. It ain't town, that's for sure."

A whimper from the third form took their attention. Then a sniffle and a question. "What do they want with us?"

Grace searched her mind for the identity of the familiar voice and settled on the storekeeper's wife. What in the world? "Mildred? Mildred Traynor?"

"Yes." Mildred sounded desperate as she continued. "Missus Polk? You too? What are we going to do? How are we—"

Grace's take-charge nature kicked in as she cut Mildred off. "Try to stay calm. Don't panic. We have to figure this out."

Rita chided back. "Yeah, good luck with that."

Movement caught Grace's eye. What appeared to be the flap of the tent was lifted away, admitting a large form. Light, she estimated to be from several fires outside, dispelled some of the darkness, identifying the form as a man. He moved closer.

"Ladies." The man spoke pleasantly, cordially. "Good evening and welcome to your new home."

Grace, thoroughly outraged, spoke up. "What is the meaning of this? Who are you and what do you want with us?"

Firelight glinted off the man's teeth as he smiled confidently. "Victor Garand, at your service. We're in need of some female assistance. You ladies will fill that bill for us."

"You're nothing but a kidnapper. You'll get no assistance from me. I demand you release us immediately and let us go. You have no right to detain us."

Garand leaned in, still smiling. "Well, you speak right up, don't you? Think twice before you incur my wrath, dear lady. I make the rights here, and I say you have none. You are my prisoners, and you will do my bidding or you'll suffer the consequences. Now, again, my name is Victor Garand, Mister Garand to you. Your attitudes will determine how well you're treated here. You'd best keep that in mind."

Grace glared at him, then she checked her temper, concerned with the fate of her two companions as well as her own.

Rita spoke up. "In that case, Mister Garand, what's your pleasure?"

Grace couldn't hold it back. "Rita!"

"Oh, shut up, missus holier-than-thou. You don't make up my mind, I do."

Garand straightened up. "You'd better bury whatever hatchets you had out for each other and settle in for the long haul or your lives will become pret-ty miserable."

Mildred broke down, sobbing uncontrollably. "Please, I just want to go home."

Garand went to her, lifting her head with a finger under her chin. He chuckled. "Why, you are home, little one."

She turned away and continued crying.

Garand looked around at Grace and Rita. "You're all home, so you might as well get used to it."

11

THREE MONTHS ON THE TRAIL, constantly heading northwest, then north, Lon and Rhiann made fifteen to twenty miles a day, camping at night or staying at nearby towns to rest more comfortably. The more mountainous terrain of northern California slowed their progress, but their determination to reach Oregon to begin a new life together never wavered.

Stalking mountain cats and hungry coyotes made their progress interesting, if not more dangerous, but Gray's constant diligence and Lon's accuracy with his Winchester kept them both safe and well fed.

Breaking camp one morning, Rhiann dumped the remnants of the morning coffee onto the campfire to extinguish the flames as Lon finished packing away their blankets on the mule. After a clear water rinse, Rhiann placed the pot into the *alforja,* the wicker basket secured to the mule's pack saddle.

"Any idea how much farther the Oregon line is?"

Lon pushed his hat back. "'Bout a week, I reckon. Hard to pin it down. You got to be getting mighty weary of this. Wisht I could ease it for you."

Rhiann shrugged. "It is what it is. We can't get there any other way but to keep riding north. I was just curious."

"I know, me too. Maybe I'm wrong. Maybe less'n a week."

She kissed him on the cheek. "We'll find out when we get there. Let's get to riding."

They mounted and struck out from the campsite across country toward the mountains. After an hour on the trail, they rounded a bend formed by an outcropping of boulders, putting them onto a fairly flat plain. Lon pulled Gray up short. "Hold up." Rhiann reined up as the mule came to a stop between them.

About an eighth of a mile forward, a tall, slim figure moved erratically in their general direction but not directly toward them. He didn't see them and appeared out of it.

Rhiann squinted to get a clearer view. "Lon, he looks—"

"He's in trouble. Stay here."

"Oh, no, where you go, I go."

Lon released the mule's reins and urged Gray forward at a trot. At almost the same time, Rhiann moved forward behind him. As they approached, now nearing a gallop, the skinny bald-headed man crumpled to the ground on his stomach and lay still. Lon dropped from the saddle and hurried the few steps to the man. Rhiann halted a few feet away and dismounted. She reached Lon as he crouched to check the man.

Semi-conscious, he gasped for breath, wheezing loudly. Lon leaned in for a better look. "He's been running hard, like somebody's chasing him." He rolled the man over and propped his head on an extended leg. "Get him some water."

Rhiann turned to her saddle and grabbed the canteen. She uncorked it and handed it to Lon.

"Easy, friend." He brought the opening to the man's parched, cracking lips. "Just a little now. You don't want to founder." He allowed a few drops to pass into the man's mouth and pulled the canteen back. Most of that was lost, but a bit went home and generated some coughing. The spasm seemed to bring the man back, and he jerked in an attempt to get up.

"Whoa, now, lay still. You ain't in no shape."

"Got to... get away." The barely audible words came through a spurt of gagging sounds.

Lon put a hand on his shoulder to restrain him. "Whoa, there. What're you running from?"

The man focused on Lon, then glanced around at Rhiann. "They're after me."

Rhiann joined Lon in the crouch. "Calm down. We'll help you."

He lay back, exhausted. Lon offered more water. It went a little smoother this time. "Who's after you?"

The answer was garbled, sounding like "walls."

Lon leaned closer. "What?'

"Rawls." This was clear and more emphatic.

Lon and Rhiann concentrated on the man and his poor condition as Gray sounded an alarm. Lon glanced around as a new sound broke the silence. Two horsemen, out of sight until clearing the rise behind them, galloped in close, pulling up sharply, both brandishing revolvers. As Lon attempted to get up, one man shouted an order, "Hold it!"

Lon stayed put. He recognized the man shouting.

Both men dismounted quickly, leveling side arms on them. Rawls stepped forward as the other man backed him up.

Taking in the scene, Rawls sported a grin. "Well, well, looks like we bagged three for one."

With no time and in no position to react, Lon glanced at Rhiann and shook his head ever so slightly, then eyed the intruders, keeping his hands in sight. Rhiann took a glimpse of the two men with guns, then trained her gaze on Lon, understanding the position of his hands to indicate he would not make a move.

She held off any action.

Rawls took another step forward. "Here's the way this is going to go. You two stay right where you roost. Lakota here's going to relieve you of your hardware. Then you're going to stand up and back away from Stretch there. One wrong move and it'll be your last."

Staying out of the line of fire, Lakota circled them, pulled their revolvers, and stepped away. Rawls made a gesture with his left hand. They got up and stepped back from Stretch. Rawls glanced at the Indian. "Get the extra mount." Lakota trotted away into the nearby bushes and emerged with a bareback horse.

Rawls pointed to Stretch. "Sling him up there."

Lakota easily lifted Stretch and draped him face down across the horse's back. The impact depleted what little wind Stretch had, generating a grunt. With a length of rope he pulled from his sash, Lakota bound the skinny man's hands to his ankles under the horse's belly to hold him in place.

Rawls never took his eyes off Lon and Rhiann. He studied Lon carefully. "Goddamn, you look like—I know you."

"Don't strain yourself, Rawls. You know me, all right."

After a moment's hesitation, Rhiann saw recognition cross Rawls's face. "Alonzo Pearce."

Lon said nothing. He just nodded.

Rawls limbered his left arm. "Arm still aches now and again."

Lon shrugged. "As I recollect it, you had a chance to back off. Should a took it."

Rhiann's mind raced to recall the account Lon told of his exploits on the Tell Ranch in Texas some years earlier, the culmination of which was a shoot-out with Rawls. Yeah, Rawls lost that one and wound up in prison. Now he had Lon in a bind, and he looked like he'd enjoy squeezing.

"You'll do the backing off this time. Now, you can ride straight up or face down like him. Your choice how, but either way, you're coming with us. How's it going to be?"

"Straight up." Lon glanced at Rhiann. She read the frustration, the resignation in his expression. They were cornered. No way out. Yet. But she trusted he would find a way. She'd defer to his judgment.

"Get up on them ponies."

When they were mounted, Rawls moved closer to Rhiann, leering at her. "Where'd you find this one? She ain't half bad."

"Joined me a piece back. Heading to Oregon to meet her husband. Wanted protection to get there."

Rawls chuckled. "Well, now, that worked out real good, didn't it?" Rhiann felt his eyes boring into her. "Yeah, she ain't half bad."

Lon's voice went low. "Leave her alone."

Rawls shot a glance at Lon. "Case you ain't noticed, you ain't in no position to mouth off, so shut it or I'll shut it for you."

Rawls and Lakota climbed on their horses and began herding their captives north. The pack mule, left behind by Lon and Rhiann, quit grazing and hustled to catch up to the only promise it had of food better than scrub grass.

THE BRIGHT SUN RESTED HIGH over the mountains in the western sky as they rode into what appeared to be a mining operation. Lon quickly tried to assess the situation and commit the lay of the land to memory. A fleeting glance at Rhiann told him her detective background had kicked in, causing her to do the same. A desperate feeling came over him as he searched for a way out of a situation he rapidly saw as less than hopeful.

Before them, mining activities were conducted under guard. A half dozen riflemen patrolled as what seemed like prisoners toiled at various duties. As they rode at a walk past a large corral, three buildings on their right were situated in a line along a slope leading to a forty foot high ridge on the north side. The first two, a long bunkhouse type structure and a newer one that looked to be a cook shack, led to a cabin with some weathering to it, giving the impression of being older.

On the left, apparatuses used in the breaking down and extraction process of gold ore lined the opposite incline. Lon recalled similar devices he'd encountered in his travels.

The relatively flat face of the huge mountainous mass at the rear of the canyon bore a shaft opening at its left corner. A road bed worn from constant use marked the route from the shaft to the equipment. A mule drawn wagon, led by a captive and laden with freshly excavated rocks, emerged from the tunnel and made its way to the closest station.

Rawls led the party to the cabin and halted the procession. Several of the workers paused to observe the newcomers, but rifle wielding guards quickly changed their minds.

The cabin door opened. A hulking man stepped out as Rawls dismounted. He joined Rawls near the horses, scanning the scene.

"He alive?" The man scrutinized Stretch.

"Just barely."

"Who are they?"

"We caught 'em trying to help Stretch. No idea about the woman, who she might be. This is Alonzo, wanted in more states'n I can name. He's the one sent me up a spell back, so I got a score to settle with him."

"Then I'm sure you'll relish working him extra hard."

Rawls flashed a grin at that.

The man studied Lon and Rhiann for a long moment. "My name is Victor Garand. This is my operation, and these people are my prisoners. Now that you're here, you are too. You'll learn very quickly to cooperate or there will be consequences." He directed his gaze to Rhiann. "And what do they call you?"

"Rhiann."

"Unusual name. You related to…?" He moved his chin toward Lon.

"No."

Rawls leaned in and spoke quietly to Garand, not low enough to prevent Lon from hearing. "Says she's traveling with him for protection to get to Oregon and meet up with her husband."

"Interesting. Needless to say that won't work out for you."

Rhiann's expression was defiant. "If I don't show up, my husband will come looking for me."

"Ah, but he won't find you. Nobody will. Nobody knows this is here. And nobody seems to care about the missing." Garand turned to Lon. "So you're a wanted man, eh? Well, it doesn't matter here. We can certainly find work for anyone, you two included. Rawls, have the women take care of Stretch. I want him in shape to work as soon as possible. I'll leave these two in your charge. Apply them appropriately." He left them and returned to the cabin.

Lon and Rhiann shot quick looks at each other.

Rawls waved his gun toward the ground. "Get down. Lakota, take Stretch and the woman to the kitchen. Tell 'em to patch him up so's he can work."

They dismounted while Lakota cut the ropes holding Stretch in the saddle. He easily shifted the semi-conscious form onto his shoulder and grabbed Rhiann's wrist. Pulling her along, he headed for the middle building. Angered by the Indian's rough treatment of Rhiann, Lon made a move to help her.

Rawls pointed the revolver at him. "You stay put." With no other option, surrounded by ready guns, Lon complied. Rawls glanced around. "Hey, Foley."

From near the shaft opening, Foley, carrying a rifle, responded to the call, taking long strides to join his friend. "Yeah?"

"Recollect that *hombre* I had that run-in with down Texas way? The one shot me and turned me over to the law?"

"Yeah."

"Well, that's him. Alonzo Pearce."

Foley flashed a grin, glaring at Lon. "Any friend a Rawls's is a friend a mine… friend."

Rawls let out an evil laugh. "Put him in the shaft. Let's see how *he* likes breaking rocks."

"Sure. Right this way, friend." Foley grabbed Lon's arm and shoved him toward the tunnel. Lon caught himself with a double step to prevent falling and continued on with Foley close behind.

The sounds of picking and digging became apparent to Lon as they entered the shaft. He tasted the dust suspended in the air because of the lack of air movement and noticed a tightness in his chest when the pollution entered his lungs. That would take some getting used to. As they moved farther in, light was supplemented by coal oil lanterns stationed on ledges scraped into the dirt walls and on flat rocks jutting from the uneven surfaces. They approached a pile of freshly excavated rocks in the center of the tunnel floor. Around it, several filthy men toiled, adding to the mound. Two others, one of them Strome, swung pick axes into the end of the shaft, chipping away chunks. The unmistakable vein of gold was in plain sight. So that was what this was all about.

Oppressive heat and stillness surrounded Lon. Foley's call to Strome stopped the man in mid swing. He lowered the pick. "What do you want?"

"Got a new one here. Show him what to do." Foley shoved Lon toward Strome. Lon stopped himself from stumbling. He glared back at Foley.

Foley sneered. "Don't look to make no moves, friend. I'd just as leave kill you as look at you."

Taking those words to heart, Lon moved closer to Strome.

"Get you an axe there. Just do what I do." Strome indicated a pick axe leaning against the shaft wall. Lon picked it up. He stopped for a second, considering turning on Foley, using the axe as a weapon. Foley's long gun leveled on him changed his mind.

"Right there." Strome pointed to a spot on the shaft end.

Lon swung the tool, sinking its pick into the hard packed dirt surrounding various size stones in the abutment. As the particles of earth fell away, he used the chisel end to remove loose stones and larger rocks. His mind raced to find a way out of this for himself and Rhiann, maybe for everyone involved. Without full knowledge of the operation, he was at a loss. As he swung the axe repeatedly, he resolved the situation would not stand. He'd gain the facts he needed and find a way out, but it would take time.

12

THE INDIAN CARRIED THE AILING Stretch effortlessly while pulling Rhiann along. No amount of effort could get her free of his grip. Halfway to the building, she stopped trying, wanting to conserve energy. She glanced around behind her to see Lon being taken to the shaft opening. What did they have in store for him? For that matter, what did they have planned for her?

Balancing Stretch on his shoulder, Lakota opened the door of the rudimentary cook shack and entered, with Rhiann still in his grasp. Three women, standing near a long table, turned to the source of the disturbance. Lakota shoved Rhiann toward them. He lifted Stretch from his shoulders and placed him roughly on the uneven floor boards.

Rhiann stopped her forward motion short before colliding with the table. She gazed at the women, taken by their disheveled appearance. The one closest to her, the blonde, had a cheap look about her, and she seemed comfortable with it. Rhiann suspected she'd developed the look long before her captivity. The older woman had come from a better upbringing, obvious by her bearing, evident even through the grime. She appeared quite uneasy being here. The third, younger one showed instant fear in the presence of the Indian. She shrank back to the far side of the table.

Lakota's deep, disturbing voice broke the silence. "Put woman to work. Fix man up for work." He turned and walked out, slamming the door behind him.

The blonde sized Rhiann up. "Well, where'd they find you?"

Rhiann hesitated, uncertain of her circumstances or the company she was in.

The older woman took a step toward her. "It's all right. We're prisoners here too."

Rhiann began to warm to her. "My… companion and I stopped to help this man on the trail. They took us prisoners before we knew they were there."

"I think you might be lucky they didn't kill you, although, considering these circumstances, perhaps not. Is Stretch hurt?"

"Not that we could tell. He just seems worn out from running." Rhiann took a step nearer and lowered her voice. "What's going on here? What is all this?"

The blonde broke in. "You'll find out in time enough. Right now there's work to be done and Stretch there to fix. Get to it."

The older woman crouched at Stretch's side. She looked up at Rhiann. "Can you help me with him?"

Rhiann joined her, glancing around to see the younger woman moving farther away and the blonde standing with her hands propped on her hips. Rhiann turned her attention to helping the ailing Stretch.

The older woman leaned in, speaking in a whisper. "My name is Grace Polk. I'm sorry you've been involved in this."

"Rhiann. It is what it is. What's wrong with him? He's not hurt. He should have come around by now."

"Stretch has a problem with his lungs. He was nearly killed in a fire a few years back. It scorched his lungs, so he can't breathe well. Any little exertion leaves him weak."

"You sound like you know him?"

"I know everyone here. We're all from Colinas de Oro. We've all been kidnapped to work here."

Rhiann leaned in, speaking lower, suspicious of the blonde's intentions. "That should mean they'll have search parties out looking for them."

Grace shook her head. "Not that town. No one seems to care about their neighbors."

Rhiann tucked the information in the back of her mind. She'd deal with it later. "What can we do for Stretch?"

"Water and rest are all that will help him." Grace got up and lifted a dipper from a nearby water bucket. Rhiann put her arm behind Stretch's neck and lifted his head. Grace applied the dipper to his lips. He slurped at it, taking in a bit, coughing and wheezing, then came around to a semblance of consciousness.

"Easy, Stretch." Grace took the dipper away. "A little at a time."

Stretch seemed more aware. He nodded weakly. Grace gave him more water, slowly, until he could drink the contents without gagging. He looked around at the faces staring at him.

"Missus Polk." Then he glanced at Rhiann. "You... where?" He looked around at his surroundings. "Oh... they brung me back?"

Grace sighed. "Yes, Stretch, you're back at the mine."

A helpless, desperate expression crossed his face. "Oh."

He turned away.

The blonde's sharp voice cut in. "Enough screwing around, ladies. You're wasting time. Get back to work."

Rhiann came to her feet, staring at the woman. "This man could be dying for all you know. What the hell is your problem?"

The blonde took a threatening step forward. "You just shut the hell up, girlie. I'm in charge here. You'll do what I tell you."

Rhiann was unmoved by the threat. "Or?"

Grace rose to place a restraining hand on Rhiann's arm, her gaze fixed on the blonde. "Don't push it, Rhiann. Rita's been put in charge of the kitchen. She can make it harder for all of us."

Rhiann hesitated. Any action on her part might come back on all of them. "All right." Her hands went out, palms down, in a submissive gesture. "All right. What do we need to do?" The question was directed to Grace.

Rita answered it. "That's better. Let him lay there. Get back to making the food."

Rhiann took a calming breath, trying to control her temper as Grace led her to the table. The other woman came to join them, still trying to fade inside herself. She wrung and fidgeted her hands, displaying her desperation. Behind them, Rita stood with her arms folded, like the overseer she professed to be. Taking into account the threat Rita posed, Rhiann deferred any further questions to a more opportune time. She'd bide her time, watch and wait.

———

THE WOMEN CONTINUED THEIR LABORS, making a rabbit stew on the fire pit behind the building. When it was finished, the huge pot required the hands and backs of two women to lug it into the kitchen. Rhiann and Grace accomplished the task, straining over the short distance to the table. Mildred tended the fire and then followed them inside. Rita opened the front door and rang what probably had been a school bell in another life, the call for work to stop for the noon meal. The other women arranged a serving line behind the long table, Rhiann following Grace's lead.

A few seconds later, Rawls entered. He was followed by Hatcher, carrying the Sharps at port arms. They stationed themselves on either side of the door. Then the captives filed in, took tin plates and spoons from the set up at the table's end, and walked past the serving table, holding out their plates. The women served from the stew pot. Rita cut the line and filled two plates, then left the cabin carrying them.

At about the middle of the line of men, Lon appeared and followed the lead of those in front of him. When he reached Rhiann, he glanced up, crossing her gaze. The shake of his head was imperceptible to those around them, but it conveyed its message to her. Maintain the pretense he'd established when they were taken. They were no more than traveling companions.

"Sorry I got you into this, ma'am."

As she ladled a portion onto his plate, she played along. "It's not your fault."

From his spot at the door, Rawls shouted. "Shut up, you two. Move along."

Lon moved on in the line, following the others outside to find a place to sit and eat.

THOSE WHO HAD ALREADY GOTTEN their food were spread out, seated on the ground between the buildings and the ore processing equipment. Others filed out of the kitchen with plates, seeking seats. Guards stood with rifles in strategic positions around the group, keeping them corralled. Lon found a spot near Strome, so far the only person he was acquainted with in this new situation. He would be as good as anyone for use in gathering information.

Lon squatted close to the man. Only then did he notice the badge still pinned to Strome's ragged shirt. It read, *Deputy Sheriff.* Sure, why not. After what he'd experienced so far this day, nothing surprised him. "Deputy, huh?"

Strome made a scoffing sound. "So what?"

They ate while they talked.

Lon spoke through a mouthful of stew. "Just I don't cotton to being a slave. Don't plan on staying around here long. I'd reckon you'd want in on a plan to get shed of this place, you being a lawman and all, 'less you got a scheme yourself."

Approaching footsteps halted the conversation. Carrying his rifle at port arms, slapping the barrel against his left palm threateningly, Paco stepped through the seated men, stopped at Lon and Strome for a second, glared at them, then moved on.

Strome waited until Paco was a few steps away. "What plan you talking about?"

"Ain't got one yet, but I will. Just a matter of time. You interested?"

"Stretch tried it. You seen what happened to him, how they brought him back. Not looking to wind up like that."

Lon studied the man. "So you're fine with being a slave here?"

Strome glared back. "I never said that. I'm biding time. What makes you figure you can do any better'n Stretch?"

"I ain't Stretch."

"That's for sure." The strange voice came from behind Lon. He looked around.

Flick, carrying a full plate, sat between them. "Just who are you?"

"Name's"—Lon still had not gotten used to using his given name. It took him a second—"Pearce."

"Mine's Flick."

Strome made a face. "Yeah, he's got the cushy job, being the assayer."

"Shut up, Strome. I've got the skills, and Garand knows it."

Lon saw an opening. "Who is this Garand *hombre,* anyhow?"

"He's the big guy runs this show. You'll find out soon enough."

Lon responded in a sarcastic sing-song tone as he scooped the last spoonful of stew. "I can't wait."

AFTER SERVING THE GUARDS AND consuming meals themselves, Rhiann, Grace, and Mildred started the cleanup. Since Rita had not returned, Rhiann took the chance to speak with her fellow captives as they worked.

"Have you thought about how we can get out of here?"

Grace answered quietly. "Constantly, but they keep such a close watch on us. These men Garand has seem like they wouldn't mind killing any of us."

"There's got to be a way. We just have to find it. Now, who's this Garand you mentioned?"

"I don't know much about him. He's a stranger. Apparently, he was a partner in this mine. He killed the other owner and was arrested for it. He escaped from jail and came back with all these men. They took over the mine and kidnapped everyone here to work it."

"What about the blonde?"

"Rita? She's a lost soul, I'm afraid. She makes her living with her body, if you take my meaning."

Rhiann nodded her understanding of the term.

Grace continued. "I've tried to help her, but she just pushes me away. She was brought here when Mildred and I were, but she seems to have found a way to make her life here easier on her own. She's taken up with Garand. She's become his confidant, so we can't trust her."

"Right, I figured that. We'll have to keep her in the dark as much as possible." Rhiann turned to Mildred, sensing the girl's fearful nature. "I know this is scary for you, but if we stick together, we can figure this out. We can help each other."

On the point of tears, Mildred spoke up. "I just want to go home. I can't stand this anymore." She broke down sobbing and covered her face with her hands.

Grace put a comforting arm around Mildred's shoulder. "Mildred came west as a mail order-bride. She's married to the storekeeper in town. Unfortunately, I don't think they're very happy. I think he's mistreating her. When she says she wants to go home, she means her home back east."

"That's a tall order." Rhiann put her hand on Mildred's upper arm as additional consolation. "Mildred, how about, for now, we concentrate on getting clear of this mess?"

Mildred nodded her head. Because of her position, her whole body mimicked the move, as if she were rocking. Her emotions got the better of her. She wept as both women tried to comfort her.

Rhiann addressed Grace. "I get the impression you're some kind of a minister."

"My husband was. He became ill and passed away a year ago. I've tried to carry on his work, but I haven't accomplished much so far. The people of Colinas de Oro are a strange breed, unconcerned with anyone but themselves."

RHIANN AND THE WOMEN SPENT the night on folding canvas cots. Rita never returned from wherever she went after supper. Rhiann guessed, from the information Grace had provided, she'd gone to eat with Garand and stayed to entertain him. Rhiann dozed a few times during the night, but restful sleep never came. Her mind raced between trying to hatch a plan of escape and concern and worry about Lon. To make matters worse, Stretch, who had been placed on one of the cots, wheezed and coughed all night.

Just after dawn, Snake burst into the kitchen carrying a lit coal oil lamp. The light and noise roused the women. Snake scanned the cots and moved quickly to Stretch as Stretch propped himself on his elbows, still groggy.

"Get your ass out a bed. You're going back to work."

Stretch tried to say something, but his cough prevented it.

Snake persisted. "I said get up."

Rhiann, throwing caution to the wind, intervened. "Can't you see he's sick? How can he work?"

Snake flashed a glare at her, pointing a finger. "You shut your mouth, lady. This ain't none a your business." He turned back to Stretch. "Come on, beanpole, move."

Reluctantly, Stretch struggled to get off the cot. He straightened up slowly. Snake stepped behind him and shoved him toward the door. Stretch stumbled but managed to catch himself before he fell. "Keep going." Snake followed the sickly man out the door.

In the low light let in the room by the open doorway, Rhiann looked across at Grace and breathed out a concerned sigh. Grace shook her head as they both got up from the cots.

At breakfast, Lon and Rhiann got a fleeting chance to flash wan smiles at each other in the chow line. He was moved along before a word could be exchanged between them, though. The women continued with kitchen cleanup and preparations for the noon meal as the men were put to work under guard. Rita returned from her overnight stay with Garand in the main cabin to oversee the day's kitchen operations.

Wary of Rita, Rhiann refrained from talking with Grace further about the mine set-up in general or escape plans in particular. She concentrated on the work to which she was assigned, electing to play a waiting game.

PUT BACK TO WORK AT the same station he occupied the day before, Lon swung the pick under Paco's watchful eye and ready rifle. Beside him, saying nothing, Strome chopped away at the wall, breaking large chunks of rock free.

At mid-morning, Paco shouted at them. "Hey, *hombres, agua.*"

Already weary, they moved slowly out of the shaft into the yard with Paco trailing. As they approached the water barrel in the middle of the open area, Lon's attention was drawn to the stamping device where rocks from the tunnel were crushed. Sounds of coughing and failed attempts at catching lost breath came from there.

In front of the apparatus, Stretch doubled over, short of breath and hacking, unable to straighten up. Snake, rifle in hand, towered over him. "Quit stalling! Get up!"

Lon finished a drink from the dipper tethered by a rope to the barrel. "Ain't fit to be working," he mumbled to no one in particular.

When Stretch failed to follow his orders, Snake shifted the rifle to his left hand and released the bullwhip from its strap on his holster. He shouted as he uncoiled the lash behind him. "I said get up!" Stretch could do no more than wheeze, remaining doubled over. Snake snapped the whip forward, laying it across Stretch's back. Stretch winced and collapsed, first to his knees, then in a ball on the ground.

The sight of the atrocity compelled Lon to react. Without concern for himself, he moved on Snake, lunging forward as Snake heaved the whip behind him for another throw. Ducking under Snake's arm, he raised his left arm to block the whip hand and smashed his right fist into Snake's chin. Snake shot back a few inches, reeling from the impact.

In his peripheral vision, Lon caught sight of several prisoners getting up, maybe to join in or seize a chance at escape. They were quickly quelled by multiple guns on all sides. As Lon moved in to finish the job, caring only to prevent Snake from meting out more punishment to Stretch, a sudden strike at the back of Lon's head stopped him cold. Sharp pain filled his head. White dazzlers danced in front of his eyes as his view became hazy. Then the black closed in. He sank to his knees, out of it. More pain followed, then oblivion.

13

CHAOS IN THE YARD DREW the women to the open kitchen door. Rhiann peered out to see Lon land a punch on Snake's chin. She shuddered at the possibility that this was an attempt to escape. He knew better than to blunder into something without thinking things through and against insurmountable odds. Her view opened to see Stretch on the ground, not moving, and prisoners gathering around curiously, while guards threatened them back. At that, Rawls stepped behind Lon and hit him in the back of the head with his rifle butt. She winced as Lon collapsed to his knees, then to his side on the ground in front of Stretch.

Concerned only for Lon, Rhiann rushed past Grace.

"Rhiann, don't—"

Rhiann bounded into the yard, paying no heed to the warning. She ran across to crouch at Lon's limp form. "Lon." She reached to roll him on his back, finding him barely conscious.

A strong hand gripped her shoulder and pulled her back. She lost balance and landed hard on her rear, her hands behind her as supports. "Get away from him." Rawls loomed over her. She glanced again at Lon to see him coming back around. Random statements from the prisoners voicing the possibility of overpowering the guards and escaping surrounded her. The sentries moved in and forced them back, quelling their resistance. Rawls and Snake trained their rifles on Lon as he moved, trying to get up.

"That's enough." Garand's command was loud as he strode from the cabin. All eyes went to him as he stopped beside Rawls. "What's this about?"

"Seems our new guest don't like watching people get their come-uppance." Rawls indicated Lon, then Stretch. "He slugged Snake for taking a whip to that slacker there."

Garand's hands went to his hips. He glanced at Rhiann, still on the ground. "What's the woman's part in it?"

"Hell if I know. She horned in when I put him down."

Aware she was in danger of jeopardizing the cover Lon had set up for them, Rhiann held her tongue.

Garand bent slightly toward her. "What is he to you?"

She thought quickly. "Nothing but a human being, same as the man beside him. I'd react the same way to anyone being put upon like that." She rose and brushed the dirt from her hands and clothing.

"Quite commendable." Garand straightened, hands still on his hips. "But it won't stand here. No one interferes. Is that understood?" He turned his head to the crowd around them and raised his voice. "Anyone who does will suffer the same punishment, man or woman." He returned his gaze to Rhiann. "I'll let you slide today, but these two need to learn their place." He indicated Lon and Stretch with a hand gesture. "A few lashes should do it. Rawls, see to it, will you?"

"Sure."

As Rawls and Snake moved in to prepare Lon and Stretch to be whipped, Grace darted out from the kitchen and pulled Rhiann away from the crowd. She whispered as they walked. "You have to back off. You'll only get yourself in trouble."

They stopped halfway back to the kitchen when Snake spoke in a loud voice, "This one's dead."

Fearing the worst, Rhiann looked around to see Snake crouching beside Stretch while Rawls shoved Lon into the yard. She breathed a sigh of relief that it was not Lon and then gave in to the sorrow of Stretch succumbing.

Garand stood in the same position, staring at Stretch. "Well, that's too bad, isn't it? But he won't be missed. He wasn't contributing much anyway." He turned and walked back to the cabin.

Appalled, Rhiann made an attempt to pull away from Grace and return to Lon. Grace renewed her grip on her arm, hauling her toward the kitchen. "Rhiann, you can't help them. You'll just make it worse. Please."

Rhiann let out a heavy sigh of resignation. She allowed herself to be pulled back into the kitchen, then turned just inside to view the event about to take place.

Still groggy, Lon was jerked to his feet by Snake and pushed into the center of the yard, his head throbbing. Instinctively, he shoved back, catching Snake on the shoulder. Rawls stepped behind Lon and planted a boot at his lower back. The push forced him forward. Dizziness caused him to trip. Rawls used the butt of the rifle against his back to force him down on his stomach, then held him down with a foot. Snake moved into position as Rawls stepped back to give him room. Lon caught a fleeting sight of the smirks of anticipation on both men's faces. Snake laid the whip across his back. The lash slit the back of his shirt and bit deep into his flesh. There was that split second delay before the pain of the slash reached him. He winced, clenching his fists, determined to fight back cries of pain. Two more flays followed, each opening a new cut, a new avenue of pain. Through clamped teeth, he allowed only almost inaudible sounds to escape him. He'd not give them the satisfaction of succumbing, focusing instead on the future when he'd have his revenge.

Snake reared back to deliver a fourth lash. Rawls spoke up. "That'll do. Don't want to cripple him. He's got to work double now to make up for Stretch. Be time for more fun down the road." Lon uttered silent thanks for the respite as Rawls raised his voice to be heard by the prisoners. "The rest of you, break's over. Get back to work."

The crowd dispersed, returning to their work stations. Snake pulled Lon to a standing position and pushed him toward the shaft. "You too. Back to work."

Rhiann stared at the bloody welts across Lon's back, showing through the slashes in his shirt. She turned away in despair, walking silently past Grace. Her fists balled up at her sides, she pushed through the hatred for her captors, the thoughts of revenge on Rawls and Snake, the concern for Lon, the pain of loss for Stretch, attempting to maintain a level head. Somehow, there was a way out of this. She had to find it.

GARAND ENTERED THE CABIN. RITA sat at the makeshift table sipping coffee. Flick, standing in a back corner working his latest assay, looked around, then quickly returned to his duties.

Garand took a seat at the table opposite Rita. "What do you know about the new woman?"

"Rhiann? Not much. She don't talk much, at least to me. They likely know I'm spying on them so they all keep quiet around me. Why?"

He picked up the cup sitting in front of him. "Her concern over the guy she was brought in with has me curious. They're supposedly just traveling together for her protection, but she acts like there's more to it than that—much more."

Rita shrugged. "Maybe they got a little cozy while they were traveling. You know, lonely nights and all?"

He took a sip from the cup. "Possible, I suppose. Maybe it's not important. Maybe it could come in handy in the future, I don't know. See what you can find out from her. Trick her if you have to. Let me know what you learn."

Rita nodded. "Okay, sure."

PREOCCUPIED WITH BOTH LON'S INJURY and ruminations about how to get them out of this mess, Rhiann went through the motions of the work assigned to the women. Neither problem could be resolved, but each distracted her. She needed a plan. Did Lon have one? She hoped so. He was better suited to slip away unnoticed and had the experience to avoid recapture while trying to bring help. She did not, but, given the chance, she'd go for it anyway and make the rest up as she went. There had to be a way....

She finished a cut through a potato with a vegetable knife, failing through lack of concentration to remove her thumb from under the blade. Contact left nothing but a mark on her finger, the dullness of the blade evident. Close. No blood drawn though. If the damn thing had been properly sharpened, who knew what the result would have been? It was enough, however, to snap her back to reality, and enough to draw Grace's attention.

"Rhiann, be careful. You might have cut yourself."

Rhiann passed it off. "This thing can't cut lard. I'm all right."

Rita stood nearby. "Thinking about your man, huh?"

That brought Rhiann back to center. She saw Rita's attempt for what it was—a probe for information for Garand. "You're wrong. He's not my man. My man is in Oregon waiting for me. Lon is just a traveling companion, protection till I get to Oregon."

Rita shook her head. "You sure made it look like you two're pretty close."

"I'd do the same for you if you were hurt. The same as I did for poor Stretch."

Rita smirked. "Uh-huh."

At supper, Lon passed Rhiann in the chow line. She purposely refrained from acknowledging him, feeling Rita's watchful eye on her from the corner where she stood. She got a good look at the cuts the whip had left on his back as he walked away. They needed tending to prevent infection. She'd have to figure a way to accomplish that and soon. Their gazes crossed as he went by. He said nothing and moved on.

As darkness beckoned, the camp settled in for exhausted sleep. Rhiann glanced out the kitchen door into the yard as Lon placed his bedroll in a slight declivity in the terrain midway between the bunkhouse and the corral. Tucking that into her memory, she took to her cot, but sleep was not her aim. While she put together a treatment plan and mentally listed the implements she'd need to care for Lon, she bided her time. It had to be late and quiet for this to work. After midnight, she rose and assembled a dish towel she hoped was clean and a jar of honey. The towel would double as a bandage. The honey was the closest thing she had to anything with healing properties. That was one of the many survival tricks she'd learned from her policeman father. She was glad she'd listened.

Trying to mimic the quietness of a church mouse, she cracked the door to the outside wide enough to scan the yard. There'd be a guard out there, hopefully tired enough to succumb to a doze. Her gaze zeroed in on Paco, the Mexican, sitting cross-legged, outlined in the moonlight. She could make out the rifle across his lap and his hat, the wide brimmed sombrero, with the crown dipped forward almost level with the ground. He appeared to be more than dozing, but she couldn't depend on that. She'd still need to be like a ghost. She slipped out and pulled the door closed, making no sound at all.

Paco was stationed across the yard at the midpoint between the mine shaft and the exit road. From this spot, he had a clear view of anything that moved on the side of the camp that housed the population. To do that, however, his eyes had to be open.

Rhiann moved carefully between the kitchen and the guards' cabin, trying to fade into the cabin wall. Rounding the back of the bunkhouse, she headed for the corral. For some reason, nobody had unsaddled the horses they'd ridden in on, simply corralling them.

Gray's reaction to strangers probably had something to do with that, preventing them from getting close. Lon kept an extra shirt in his saddle bag. She'd need that. Stopping at the fence, she waited until the horses accepted her presence. When they'd settled down, she took a chance.

"Gray." The harsh whisper went unnoticed by the stock and un-challenged by Paco. Good. In a second, Gray rustled through the other horses and sidled up to his master's familiar companion, making low sounds of greeting. Rhiann patted Gray's neck and reached into the saddle bag. Thankfully, the shirt was on top. Her fingers brushed past the hidden gun in there, Lon's old Navy Colt. Should she? She paused for a second, contemplating taking the gun, but thought better of it. With no solid plan to go with it, and no foolproof place to hide it, the gun was of no use and could be a detriment. Discarding the idea, she pulled out the shirt and tossed it over her shoulder. Another pat on Gray's neck and she was on her way to the dip in the yard's open area where the prisoners slept.

Lon had chosen that spot intentionally, possibly with escape in mind. The section was low enough to partially obscure him from Paco's view. That would help hide her as well.

Behind her, Gray let out a nicker, louder than earlier. It had an urgency to it. Rhiann dropped to the ground and glanced over to catch Paco stirring. She froze. He moved slightly but then settled back down. She let out a sigh of relief, silently thanking Gray for the warning, and lifted herself to a crouch.

Approaching, she made out Lon's hat in the moonlight. She'd seen it enough to know it anywhere. It was on the ground next to him. He was on his stomach, uncovered, shirt off. She took a knee at his side and set the honey jar on the ground in front of her.

Rhiann's hand went to Lon's head as she leaned in close to whisper to him. "Lon." Her hand stroked his hair. He roused, eyes opening and settling on her face. She kissed him quickly, more to keep him from giving an alarm than anything else. "Shhh. Quiet." She kept her voice at the lowest whisper.

"What're you doing?" His whisper level equaled hers.

"Those cuts need tending. Can you sit up?" She picked up the jar and opened it, careful to keep the tin cap from making noise, as Lon moved to a sitting position. "Don't cry out." She coated the towel with honey and placed it over the whip cuts. "Hold this here." He reached for the ends of the towel and held them in place, wincing as the material touched the open wounds. Rhiann picked up the ripped shirt beside his hat. A twig snapped under her foot as she moved, stopping everything for a second. They both froze, waiting it out, the tops of their heads just above the ground level. She glanced at Paco, waiting for his reaction. None came.

Wrapping the shirt over the towel, she used the sleeves to tie it off across his chest, securing the makeshift bandage. She handed him the fresh shirt. "Any ideas how we can get out of this?"

He shook his head as he slipped into the shirt. "Not yet. Can't trust nobody here. Got to be on our lonesome, maybe not even together. Whoever can get clear goes for help. Bring back a posse and bust this thing up." He returned to his sleeping position.

Rhiann nodded. "Right. Got to go. Be careful." She kissed him quickly. Another twig cracked as she stepped on it. They hesitated a second before she moved again.

"You too."

Returning without incident to the kitchen cabin, Rhiann put the honey jar in its place and moved silently to her cot. She lay there, confident Lon didn't do things without thorough thought. She also was sure he had something in mind, some kind of escape plan. The sleep spot he'd chosen was not random. It hid him from the view of the guards. Maybe he'd slip away—

"Where'd you go?" Rita's harsh whisper from the adjoining cot split the quiet like a knife's edge, breaking Rhiann's train of thought.

"I couldn't sleep. I got some air, if it's any of your business."
"Everything's my business. Keep that up, you'll get yourself shot."
Rhiann turned on her side. "As you can see, I didn't."
"Yeah, this time."

14

BREAKFAST TIME THE NEXT MORNING found Rita carrying two full plates from the kitchen cabin to Garand's quarters. She used her foot to knock on the door. Garand opened it to admit her. She crossed to the small table and set the plates down, speaking quietly, but intently. "Got to talk to you." She tossed her head toward Flick who worked at the assaying station in the far corner.

Garand sat across from her. "Flick." He waived a hand at the door. "Outside a minute."

Flick turned from his work. "If I don't time this process exactly, I'll have to start it all over."

"Then you'll start it over. Just get out. Now."

Flick shrugged and crossed to the door, letting himself out.

Garand leaned over the table. "What?"

"Rhiann. After we went to bed, she went outside, about midnight, I guess. She was gone for a few minutes. I called her on it. She said she couldn't sleep and went out for some air."

"Do you believe her?"

"I guess…. She came right back, didn't try to get away."

"Why didn't the guard stop her?"

"I don't know. Maybe he was asleep."

Garand stroked his jaw. "All right. Keep a close eye on her, on all of them. Let me know anything that seems suspicious. Send Rawls in here when you're done eating. I don't like the idea of those guards not reacting." He turned his head toward the door and called over his shoulder. "Flick, get back in here."

TRYING TO ADJUST TO THE uncomfortable bandage on his back, Lon approached the tunnel to begin the day's work under the watchful eyes and rifles of the sentries. Rawls moved to stand in his path, blocking him.

"New shirt?"

Lon sneered. "Ain't new. Just ain't in pieces."

"Where'd it come from?"

Lon quickly tired of this pain-in-the-ass. "Had it in my saddlebag." He took a step to move on.

Rawls put a firm hand on Lon's shoulder to stop him. "You don't get it, do you? You're a prisoner, just like I was, thanks to you. Next time you ask, ask nice-like, or you'll get more a Snake's whip. You got that?" Rawls poked a finger in Lon's chest for effect.

Lon nodded. "Yeah, I got it. We done here?"

"We're done when I say we're done. You get this straight, Pearce, we need every man's back to get this gold out, so I'm letting you slide. Come a day when you and me'll have us a reckoning. Heap a payback coming your way."

Lon glared at the man. "Anytime. Ready and willing."

Rawls hesitated for a second, then swung a poorly aimed punch at Lon, catching him on the jaw, a glancing blow that Lon had seen coming. He rolled with it and recovered without faltering. Rawls rested his hand on the butt of his holstered revolver, a silent warning. Lon stuffed the retaliation he promised himself. That would happen when protective guns were somewhere else and the match was even. Instead, he rubbed the spot on his jaw and nodded, staring intently. "Come a day." He started again toward the shaft, stepping around Rawls.

ON HER RETURN TO THE kitchen, Rita reexamined the events of the previous night, recalling the slight noise she had heard prior to Rhiann's exit. The same sound had occurred on her return. While Rita couldn't see it in the dark of the room, she did pinpoint the sounds to the area behind the long food preparation table. There were shelves back there. Rhiann had taken something from the shelves and put it back later. What did she take, and what did she do with it?

Scrutinizing the objects on each shelf, Rita found nothing missing, nothing out of place. Wait, the honey jar. It was only about half full. She was almost willing to bet there'd been more in it the day before. Maybe almost full. That was probably it. But what the hell did she do with it? No sense guessing.

"Hey, you." She pointed at Rhiann.

Rhiann looked up from her work at the table with Grace and Mildred beside her. She made no reply.

"That little walk you took last night, that was more than just a walk, wasn't it? What the hell did you do with half a jar a honey?"

Rhiann took a moment, then came out with it, taking slow, measured steps toward Rita as she spoke. "What do you want to hear, Rita? What do you want me to say? That I took the jar of honey and went to find the man they whipped? That I slathered honey on his wounds and bandaged them to keep them from getting infected? All right, yeah, that's what I did. And I'd do it again, for anyone else here as well, even you. Maybe all of you are content to let people die, but I'm not. Is that what you want to hear?"

Rhiann's threatening approach backed Rita up a step. She needed to regroup, to regain the upper hand. "Hey, you don't get to decide shit like that. You follow orders here, nothing more. Pull something like that again and I'll—"

Rhiann took another step. "You'll what? You'll tell Garand? You'll turn me in?" She came within two steps of contact with Rita. "You go right ahead. Tell him, and while you're at it, tell him I'm actually helping him by keeping that man alive so he can work. Go on and tell him, but prepare yourself, lady, for what comes back on you when you do, 'cause I swear to you, it will come, and I will bring it."

Rita blurted her response without a thought. "You'll never pull that off."

Rhiann was steadfast. "What're they going to do, kill me? They'll kill us all when they're done with us anyway. They can't afford not to. Just remember this, you cross me and you'll never see it coming."

Now fear suddenly mixed with her anger, and Rita could not find the sand to retaliate. "I'm just telling you to watch your step, that's all. He's a little loco, you know."

"Oh, I know very well he's unbalanced. He has to be to be doing what he's doing. What I'm telling you is don't underestimate me, and stay the hell out of my way."

Rita had not expected such a forceful pushback. She took the path of least resistance. "Okay, look, I'm just going to drop it. We'll just drop it for now."

Rhiann nodded, seething. "Yeah, that works for me. For now."

IN THE MIDDLE OF THAT night, Lon lay prone in his bedroll, favoring his injured back. Purposely positioned in the little declivity where Rhiann had dressed his wounds, and purposely awake, he listened carefully, focusing on the night creatures' calls and the sleep sounds around him. No one stirred. It was time. Taking his hat, he rose quietly, crouching, and scanned the area for the guard. It wasn't

Paco. The absence of that big *sombrero* confirmed that. He couldn't tell who it was, but it looked like sleep had found him. He looked around to see he was in line with the end of the bunkhouse. If he could make it to there, the spot would offer concealment from the guard's view. He could navigate from there. He'd pondered this during the day while working, deciding this attempt was worth the risk.

He rolled out of the blankets and went to a low crawl, almost even with the ground so he'd present the smallest image. He gambled the guard would not notice the movement. It was only a few feet, but it seemed endless as he elbowed and kneed his way along. He struggled to keep his efforts quiet as he continued the crawl until he reached the building. Hauling himself around, he leaned against the bunkhouse wall, took a second to catch his breath, and rose to his knees, ready to move. Step one done.

On shaky limbs, he peered out to scan the yard, checking on the guard. Still in place. A horse whinnied in the near distance. Gray? Might could be if he caught his master's scent.

In the middle of the yard on the machinery side, the lone guard sat cross-legged with a rifle across his lap. Lon still could not make out who it was, but the figure was big. His next move had to be done quiet, fast, and from behind the man if it was going to work. The way he figured to do it would take a while, but that didn't matter. There'd be plenty of darkness for hours to come.

He took to the ground again, low crawling across the rough surface of the yard, staying below the rise of the ground dip. The horse made a noise again when he was halfway across. Yeah, that was Gray. The guard, now roused, glanced over at the corral. Lon hugged the ground and stayed completely still. He waited, giving the disturbance a minute to settle.

He peeked across as the guard looked away, then completed the crawl and came to a crouch at the beginning of the south hill slope. A glance at the guard told him he was far enough behind the man to stay out of his peripheral vision. The low light would help with that. Staying crouched, he moved up the grade slightly, then turned toward the man, staying directly above him.

Directly behind the guard, Lon was now able to determine he'd be up against the Indian, Lakota, adding the need for another layer of stealth. Lon moved forward carefully. This had to be done smooth and silent, a practice he'd developed over the years. He moved into position, clasped both hands together, and brought them down hard on the back of Lakota's neck. The Indian grunted, a noise sounding like a cough, and slumped forward. Lon leaned in, grabbing the rifle at both ends. Pulling the weapon hard under Lakota's chin, he lifted the man to a sitting position. The pressure on Lakota's throat cut off his breath. Stunned as he was from the sudden blow, he put up only a light struggle as he gurgled for air. Lon pulled harder. Lakota's hands flailed about, attempting resistance but accomplishing nothing. Lon held the rifle in place until Lakota's head dropped forward and his body went limp. Releasing the hold, Lon allowed the man's body to slip to the ground. Was he out cold or dead? Lon didn't check. Didn't matter, as long as he was out of the way.

Setting the Winchester aside, Lon unbuckled Lakota's gun belt and pulled it away from his body. Now he had a rifle and a side arm and shells for both. Step two done.

He strapped on the pistol belt, then picked up the long gun and his hat. A twig snapped under his foot. He crouched and froze, waiting several seconds for a reaction. It never came. He rose and hurried toward the corral. To get there, he had to pass the sleeping prisoners and the bunkhouse again. He bent low and moved at a trot, making as little noise as possible, trying to maintain a low profile while keeping an eye on the door and the captives. His luck held. He had no idea why, and he wasn't questioning it. No movement came from the door, and no alarm was sounded by those asleep on the ground. Almost there.

Reaching the corral fence, he found Gray waiting for him. Affectionate nickers greeted him. He responded with comforting pats on the neck and nose. He'd noticed much earlier the fact that they hadn't unsaddled Gray. The horse likely had something to say about attempts to do so, finding the approach of strangers distasteful and the presence of particularly menacing ones a reason to raise hooves in defense. That'd change anyone's mind. In point of fact, although uncomfortable for the horse, it saved Lon the time and effort of saddling up before his departure, or riding bareback. Taking Gray's lead line, he walked the horse along the fence to the gate, swung it open, and led Gray out. He made no effort to close the gate. If it afforded the horses inside the means to wander off, so much the better. Anything slowing down a pursuit was welcome. Holding Gray to a slow walk to keep the noise down, he made his way up the road to the approach trail several yards away. Then he swung up into the saddle and kicked up a gallop, heading east.

A SHORT TIME LATER, RAWLS stepped out of the bunkhouse lighting a hand rolled cigarette. As he took a draw, instinctively scanning the area before him, he was instantly aware things were out of place. The corral gate was wide open. Horses wandered about, grazing, inside and outside the corral. A quick glance to his right revealed the clumped form on the ground. Lakota, not sleeping, not in that position. Rawls flicked the smoke and trotted across the yard, stopping at the Indian's body. "Lakota, what the hell?"

No movement. Rawls heaved a foot into Lakota's midsection. Lakota grunted, then came to a sitting position, clutching his throat.

Rawls leaned in. "What the hell happened?"

The Indian growled to clear his throat and engage his voice. "Choked… blacked out." His voice was a harsh whisper.

"Shit." Rawls glanced around. "Somebody got out."

Rawls headed for the bunkhouse on a dead run. "Roll out in there. We got trouble."

Foley met him at the door, hitching his gun belt. "What?"

"Somebody got away." Rawls tossed his head in the Indian's direction as Lakota struggled to stand on shaky legs. "Throttled Lakota and took off."

By now, a few of the men had spilled out. Others appeared in the doorway in various states of dress. They bunched up and headed toward Lakota. The Indian met them halfway across the yard.

Rawls reached him first. "Who was it?"

Lakota shook his head. "Not see." He glanced around. "Took guns."

"How long back?"

Lakota shook his head again.

Rawls flashed a disgusted look and turned to Drawden. "Get the prisoners up. Find out who's missing." He focused on Foley. "Saddle two good nags. Get ready to ride."

Foley and Drawden left the group to carry out their duties as Rawls hurried to Garand's cabin. His heavy pounding on the door brought a sleepy-eyed Garand to the doorway, hiking up trousers, displaying an inquisitive expression.

"What's going on?"

"Somebody got out."

"Who?"

"We're checking now." Rawls pointed to the crowd of prisoners forming in the center of the yard. Garand joined him. They moved quickly toward the group.

Drawden stepped away to meet them. "Your friend, that Pearce *hombre*. His ride's gone too."

"He ain't no friend. I'd just as leave kill him as look at him." Rawls glanced toward the corral. "Shit. Where's Foley with them horses? We got to get after him."

Garand gave it a second's thought. "Rawls, wait. What do you know about this Pearce?"

"I know he's like a mountain cat. Gets his teeth into something, he don't let go for nothing."

"That tells me he won't just disappear. He'll be back to finish this, if for no other reason than that woman. And no telling who or what he'll bring back with him. Send someone else to chase him down. I want you to find me more men, at least a dozen. I want a perimeter set up around the hills here to keep that bastard or anyone he brings with him the hell out."

"Ain't going to be easy, finding men like that."

"That's your problem. Get going, and do it fast if you value your stake in this operation."

Rawls hesitated. This just got more complicated than he was comfortable with, but Garand was right. If Pearce got clear, and there was a good chance of that, he'd likely bring back a posse that could overrun the camp and break up the operation and screw them out of the gold. "Drawden, you ride with Foley. Run that son-of-a-bitch down. Red, you're in charge here." He started for the corral.

Garand shouted after him. "Don't drag your feet."

Rawls shouted something unintelligible in response. At the corral, he stopped Foley. "Drawden's riding with you. Pick up his trail and stay on him. Watch your asses. He's a tricky bastard. Mess him up good, but, for sure, keep him alive. Rest a these birds needs to see what'll happen if they try it."

Foley nodded, leading two saddled horses out of the corral. Rawls lifted a saddle and blanket from the fence and sought out his mount.

15

GRAY RAN FLAT OUT FOR a good five miles before Lon pulled up on the reins. "Whoa, boy. We got to pace ourselves. Take a blow." They'd entered some foothills southeast of the mine, offering some cover to their tracks and decent concealment should it be necessary. It was still dark. They'd be out tracking him sure enough, wouldn't leave that hanging, but even good trackers found darkness a deterrent. His plan was simple. He'd stomp around in these hills for a time, over rough, hard-to-track ground, come out a few miles away to break up the trail more, then head for that town a couple of the prisoners had mentioned, Colinas de Oro, to scare up some help.

Meantime, Gray needed a proper rest. While they had no water, he had the ability to stop, well hidden, and allow Gray to catch his wind and graze on the meager grass growing through the rocks. He dismounted and pulled the saddle off. The saddle that had been in place since the morning they were taken. As Gray took advantage of the respite, Lon found some jerky in his saddle bag, as well as the old Navy Colt he kept there for emergencies, and the amnesty paper signed by Governor Wallace. "Good boy, Gray, you made them keep their distance and protected that stuff." He sat a few moments and chewed off some jerky.

The downtime brought Rhiann to mind. Sure, she was capable

enough. Hell, she'd saved his life, hadn't she? But she was alone there now. Rawls's men were hardcases, every one. He still wasn't sure how much down and dirty dealing she'd had with their likes in her Pinkerton days. She tended to talk more in the here and now than in the back then, so that was fuzzy. He'd have to remedy that if she pursued her intent to open a detective agency in Oregon. He reckoned there were plenty of Rawls's kind up there. He had to be sure she could handle it, or he'd have to step in. Might not sit so well with her. But all that was for another time. Now, he had to get her clear of Garand's crazy plan. Maybe blow the whole thing apart if he could. Whatever he did had to be quick. He saddled Gray again. "Time we pushed on, boy."

Gray's surefootedness threaded their way through the rocks for long enough to make following next to impossible. Lon directed the horse back onto a grassy flat, staying off anything that resembled a road. At that point, he was far enough away that even if they cut his trail again, they'd never connect the two as being one. He headed east for the town.

The roundabout ride took him within sight of Colinas de Oro as dawn dispelled darkness. He pulled Gray up on a slight knoll and strained his gaze to get the lay of the land. Typical small village, much the same as many cow towns he'd been in, geared to commerce more than neighborly living. The name said it all, Colinas de Oro or Hills of Gold—here to make as much off the profits from the mining trade as possible. He ciphered they'd be willing to help rescue their friends in danger, but that would be determined at the asking. Touching his heels to Gray's flanks, he moved on, hoping this would work.

The sun came up at his back as Lon entered the dusty main street of the town. Not a soul could be seen. Likely too early for any activity. Halfway in, a water trough beckoned. If he was thirsty, Gray had to be dry as a bone. He pulled up there and dismounted. "Drink your fill, boy." The horse didn't need a second invitation. Lon joined him, scooping a handful of the liquid to drink and to splash in his face.

When they were satisfied, Lon checked the length of the street from west to east, both sides, a habit he'd developed while on the run to head off questions and trouble.

Movement down at the end caught his eye. The east end boasted a livery, the probable source of grain for Gray and the possible source of information for him. Slight movement and vague noises told him somebody was there. He led Gray toward it.

In the first stall, as Lon approached, a scrawny little man with a whiskered pushed-in face and sparse hair under a dirty straw hat placed a feedbag on a small sorrel's head. The man paid no heed to his visitor's arrival until Lon spoke up. "How do."

That got his attention. He turned. "Howdy, young feller. Help you with something?" His question came in a high-pitched scratchy voice.

"Feed for Gray here and a mite a information, if you please."

"Feed'll cost you two bits. T'other's free."

Lon rummaged in the bottom of his saddle bag and came out with the requested amount. The liveryman placed the coin in the pocket of his grimy shirt. He tilted his head, indicating Lon should follow him into the shack-like building. He did, leading Gray. When the oats were in a feed bag, Lon took it and slipped it over Gray's head. As the horse munched loudly, Lon turned to the old man.

"So, young feller, what sorta information you hankering after?"

"Well, for starters, who's in charge in this town?"

The man stroked his stubbly chin as if thinking about it. "Reckon that'd be Rufus Chibnall, him being the mayor and all."

"Where'll I find this Mister Chibnall?"

"Well, sir, you'll find him at the bank up the street there, when he's there, which ain't for"—he reached inside his apron to a pants pocket and pulled out a pocket watch—" bout three hours, give or take."

"Thank you kindly, friend. Any place I can light and wait it out?"

"Naw. No place open yet awhile. You're welcome to cool your heels right here, you're a mind, seeing you stay outta my working way."

Lon pointed to a secluded corner. "I can do that, sir. Much obliged." He dropped to his butt, knees up, leaned his injured back carefully against the wall, folded his arms, and closed his eyes. He was asleep in seconds.

"RECKON YOU'LL WANT TO WAKE up now, young feller." The old man's voice was distant at first, until the sound brought Lon awake in a start. Then it snapped him back to reality when it continued. "Just seen Rufus opening up the bank."

Lon rolled to his feet, running his hand over his face. "Thanks." He looked around to find Gray standing by close to the entrance.

The stableman absently filled a feed bag as he spoke. "Say, that's quite some horseflesh you got there."

Lon walked to Gray. "Surely is. I'm thankful to have him." He picked up the dropped reins, patted Gray's nose, and led the horse into the street. "Much obliged."

"Yes, sir. Come again."

Walking the dirt street, Lon scanned the buildings to locate the bank, a small structure a few doors from Taylor's Saloon. He crossed to the hitch rail in front and tied Gray off there in the company of another saddle horse and a pack mule loaded with mining equipment. He entered the place. Unpainted clapboard walls and cheap furniture greeted him. In the back, a wire teller's cage enclosed an overweight, white-haired man in a crisp white shirt, brocade vest, and green celluloid eye shade. In front of the cage, a grimy middle-aged man scooped up cash from the ledge and turned away to leave. Lon passed him as he went to the opening in the cage. The teller met him with a forced attempt at a smile.

"Morning, stranger." His voice had a sneering, tired sound to it. He seemed pretentious, even phony, but then he was a banker.

"Morning. Tell me where I might find Mister Rufus Chinball?"

"It's Chib*nall,* mister. That's me." He seemed a tad offended.

"Oh, sorry. I'm told you're the mayor a this town."

"You were told right. What can I do for you?"

"Well, sir, name's Pearce. I just broke out of a place about ten mile west a here, a mining operation that's got a bunch of folks held as slave workers. Reckon if you might could get a posse together, we can ride out there and free them folks. They's a lot of 'em from this town. Maybe all of 'em. They's one *hombre* died already. Likely be more if they ain't stopped what they doing."

Chibnall studied Lon carefully, not saying a word.

"Mister Chibnall, you hear what I said?"

"Why, yes, I heard you. Tell me, why come to me? Why not go to the law?"

" Cause I know the law ain't here. The deputy's out there being put upon like all the rest. I worked right alongside a him till I got shed a the place."

"So that's where he got to. I wondered about that. Truth be told, he hasn't been much of a lawman since the sheriff put him here. Only made one decent arrest so far, that miner that murdered his partner, and he couldn't hold him more'n a few days before the fellow escaped."

"Might that fellow be named Garand?"

"Yes, Garand. You know him?"

"Of a sort. He's the *hombre* running the mine. Now, look, we going to get that posse up and ride out there?"

Chibnall became pensive. "Well, now, I don't know. That's really the law's job."

"Already told you the law ain't helping." Lon found this tiresome.

Chibnall pondered for a second. "There's the sheriff, over to the county seat. I think he should handle this. I really can't ask our citizens to risk their lives in a posse. We don't know anything about that sort of thing."

"I can tell you everything you need to know. I've rode in enough posses in my time. Every minute we wait, them folks is in danger. We got to get to moving."

Chibnall took a moment to consider. "I'll tell you what I'll do with you, Mister, eh… Pearce, is it? I'll dispatch a rider over to Ironsight this very day to fetch the sheriff back. It's only a two-day ride. Then the law can handle this proper."

Lon became frustrated. It showed. "Already told you, they ain't time for that. We got to go now. Ain't you concerned for your neighbor folks?"

Chibnall became defensive. "Why, of course I am. They're my friends. But I'm not going to go running off half-cocked on some wild goose chase and maybe get half of the town killed on the strength of—"

Lon was aghast. "Wild goose chase? What the hell—"

"Now, look here, I've already told you what I'm going to do. That will have to suffice. Why don't you go on up the street and get some breakfast? It'll be on the town. Here, I'll write you out a voucher." Chibnall picked up a pencil. "Then you can be on your way."

"Reckon you can shove that voucher up your ass, *Mister* Chibnall."

"Young man, there is no call to be rude—"

"Yeah, there is. A heap a call. Where'd you say that sheriff's at?"

"Ironsight, southeast of here about two days on horseback—"

Lon turned away and started for the door. "Thanks for nothing. I'll surely let that sheriff know how obliging you been."

"Mister Pearce, be reasonable. There's no need—"

"The hell there ain't." Lon glared at the man, prepared to unload on him, then he thought better of it. No time. The look of contempt he flashed would have to do. He exited quickly, pulled the reins free, swung up on Gray, and raced out of town, turning southeast as he cleared the last building.

———

RAWLS HAD BEEN GONE FOR two days in his search for reinforcements. He led six strangers past Drawden's long gun into the mine camp to be greeted by Garand meeting them on foot. Rawls drew up in the center of the yard. The six grouped in behind him.

Garand looked them over as he approached. "Are they all you could find?"

Rawls dismounted. "I's lucky to find these boys not a day's ride northeast. Rode with a couple of 'em a spell back. They'll do the job."

Garand nodded acceptance. "They'll have to. Have them settle in."

Rawls turned to the men. "Get on down, boys. Take a blow."

"Lige! That you?" Red's shout drew attention to him as he exited the shaft. The instant grin lit up his face. The quickness in his step brought him closer to a tall, white-haired member of the new group. The man reacted to the encounter gleefully.

"Red, you old son-of-a-bitch, what's it been, years?"

Red shook the man's hand vigorously. "Mighty well told. What you doing here?"

"Ask Rawls. He signed us on. Shit, it's good to lay eyes on you."

"You can say that again." Red continued shaking Lige's hand. "What's the chances?"

"Slim and none, I'd say. Hey, we got to have a drink to celebrate."

Rawls interrupted. "Leave that till later. You boys get your gear stowed. Red, show 'em where."

Red ushered the new group away, his hand on Lige's back, as Garand pulled Rawls aside.

"Keep a lid on them. They're no good to us drunk."

"Aw, they're all right. What can a few drinks hurt? It'll keep the boys from getting antsy."

"See it's held to a few."

THAT NIGHT, AN IMPROMPTU GATHERING around a campfire in the center of the yard featured the free-flow of whiskey as old friends rejoined and caught up with activities in their respective lives.

Paco popped his head in the door of the kitchen. Rhiann looked around at the intrusion to see the man's unsteadiness, obviously already under the influence.

"Hey, *muchachas, ven aquí.*" His speech was slurred. "You serve us the drinks, eh?"

He waited there as none of the women responded to the call. His grin disappeared. "Hey, you come now."

Rhiann stepped forward, intending to ease a possible confrontation before it got out of hand. "I'll go."

Wavering, Paco pointed to Mildred. *"Y usted.* You, too, *niñita."*

Mildred shrank back, fearful.

Rhiann stepped in front of Mildred, facing Paco. "You don't need her. I can handle it."

Paco shook his head, scowling. "She comes too."

Mildred relented, moving to join Rhiann. Paco stepped back to allow the women to exit into the yard. He pushed them toward the group and then squatted, almost falling at the fire.

Rhiann squeezed Mildred's hand and whispered to the frightened girl. "Just pour the drinks. Stay as far away from them as you can."

Holding liquor bottles, the women stood by at the beck and call of the steadily drunker men as they retold old stories and demanded more whiskey. Paco raised an empty cup. *"Mas, chiquíta."* Rhiann responded to Paco's slurring demand, recognizing the Mexican's increasing inability to control his actions as he succumbed to the effects of the alcohol.

Paco slumped forward in a semi-conscious state. Rhiann watched his cup fall from his hand, hitting the ground. A fleeting opportunity presented itself. With little consideration, she'd go for it. She crouched and put the bottle aside, pretending to pick up the cup, putting her in close proximity to the Mexican's sidearm.

She had shied from squirreling away Lon's Navy Colt since she had no hiding place for it. Now that Lon had escaped, things were different. She'd take the chance now to have the advantage of a defensive weapon available. As she reached her right hand to the cup, her left swiftly lifted the gun from its holster and slipped it into her skirt pocket in an almost imperceptible move. When she rose with the cup in one hand and the bottle in the other, the revolver settled into the pocket, obscuring it from view.

Giving no indication to anyone of the occurrence, Rhiann, with Mildred, continued serving drinks and dodging straying hands. Her mind raced to find an opportunity to put the weapon into play, one that would turn the tables on this drunken crew and possibly start a prisoner revolt. At the same time, Mildred's presence put the young girl in the position of becoming the pawn in a struggle for control that could endanger her life. Without tipping her hand, Rhiann could see no way to extricate Mildred from the scene. Stymied, she cursed under her breath. This would have to wait.

Rawls called a slurring halt to the proceedings a short time later. The women were dispatched back to the kitchen. Now it fell to Rhiann to find a hiding place for the iron. As she prepared for bed, her foot settled on a loose floor board, one she'd noticed some time earlier. Unseen, she worked the toe of her boot against its edge, lifting it slightly. If it gave enough, she might be able to slip the revolver beneath it. She reclined on the cot, waiting until the others were asleep. When she was sure, she rose and picked up the board, finding it hadn't been nailed down. She pulled the gun from her pocket and set it on the cross member supporting the floor, then replaced the board. Now she'd need to concoct another plan for the weapon's use. The protection it represented far outweighed the possibility of it being discovered missing.

Dawn brought an abrupt reckoning of the previous night's activities. Foley swung the kitchen door wide and shouted for the women to join the assembled group in the yard. As Rhiann and her companions stepped outside, it was clear to her from the sight of the prisoners having been herded into the yard under many guns, something was amiss. Garand, with Rita at his side, stood facing Rawls, his fists clenched at his side, an intense scowl on his face.

"I warned you about the drinking." He shouted so the entire group could hear. "I knew something like this would happen. Now, you control these men and their habits. And get rid of the liquor. It has no place here."

Rawls, clearly uncomfortable, made a feeble attempt to defend his position. "But that cost me—"

"I don't give a damn, Rawls. I didn't ask you to buy it. Dump it. Or I will."

Rawls reluctantly nodded compliance.

Garand turned his attention to the prisoners. "A guard's gun is missing. I want it back. You've got one minute to comply or you'll all face the consequences." He waited. No one moved. The prisoners glanced at each other, curious who the offender was. Garand concentrated his gaze on the women. Rhiann and Grace met his stare full on. Mildred cast her eyes away, toward the ground.

At the end of what must have been Garand's estimate of a minute, he spoke again. "All right, you've had your chance to end this peacefully. Now, surrender that gun or I'll kill a prisoner every five minutes until you do." He took the revolver from Rawls's holster and moved slowly toward Mildred. "You'll be first." She shrank back.

Struck by fear, Mildred glanced around for nonexistent help. Garand cocked the piece and aimed it at her.

Rhiann weighed the alternatives. Give up the gun or be the cause of Mildred's death. Certain of Garand's determination, she saw no other choice. "Wait."

Garand looked at Rhiann, but the gun remained aimed at Mildred. "You have something to say?"

Rhiann raised her hands palms out in a gesture of submission. "Don't hurt her. I took the gun."

Garand kept the revolver trained on Mildred. "Bring it here."

"It's in the kitchen."

"Go ahead. If you make one wrong move, your friend here is dead and so are you."

Resigned, Rhiann went back into the kitchen and fetched the revolver, careful to replace the loose board for possible future use. She walked out carrying the gun butt forward. Paco hurried to her and ripped it from her hand, shoving her at the shoulder. She caught herself as she was pushed to the side, then finished the walk to where the women stood.

Garand relaxed the hammer and handed the gun back to Rawls. He walked to where Rhiann stood, close enough to reach her. Without warning, he swung an open hand against her cheek in a stinging slap that moved her a foot back. Her hand went to the affected area, then she slowly straightened and locked eyes with Garand.

His warning came with an intense glare. "Try something like that again and you'll pay with your life."

16

RUNNING AT TOP SPEED, GRAY'S long strides ate up the miles between Colinas de Oro and Ironsight. Lon stopped at intervals, only long enough to graze and water Gray and to take care of his own basic needs. Then they were back on the trail, shortening the two-day trip to a grueling day and a half.

It was just after the noon hour when he entered the main street of Ironsight, a town similar to the one he'd just left, but larger and better developed. Based on the presence of non-mine related businesses and the lack of a front-and-center assay office, he guessed Ironsight to be less dependent on miners' trade.

He slowed Gray to a walk as he surveyed building fronts for signs of the law. Approaching an intersection, he caught sight of a structure, second in a string on the side street, bearing a sign identifying it as the sheriff's office. Under the bold, black lettering on the clapboard fascia, smaller print read, *County Clerk.* Lon directed Gray to the hitch rail in front and dismounted wearily. On a hunch, he fished the amnesty paper from his saddle bag and slipped it inside his shirt, just in case.

Randomly, hunger took hold of his mind as his belly growled noticeably, but that would have to wait. He draped the reins over the rail and stepped up on the boardwalk, hoping for better results than his encounter in Colinas del Oro.

A dark-haired, stocky man with a pencil-thin mustache sat behind a beat-up wooden desk across the room as Lon entered. He looked up, acknowledging Lon's presence with a slight nod. Lon stopped in front of the desk, giving the man a once-over, taking note of the badge on his vest. The nameplate identified the man, *Alex Martín, County Sheriff.*

"How do, Sheriff."

"What can I do for you, stranger?" His voice was smoky and gave the attitude of an impatient, busy man. His eyes told a different story as they scrutinized Lon.

"I need you to get up a posse."

"Oh, do you?" The sheriff hesitated, completing his inspection of the visitor. "Mind telling me the why of it?"

"They's an *hombre* name a Garand at a mine a few miles west of Colinas de Oro. He's holding some folks as slave labor to work the mine. Need you and a posse to make that right."

The sheriff thought for a moment while Lon found himself fed up with repeating the same story.

"Colinas de Oro, you say. One of my deputies is assigned there. You'll have to see him about this." Sheriff Martín lowered his eyes to continue scanning wanted posters in front of him.

"Sheriff, your deputy can't help. He's one a the prisoners. Already talked to the mayor in that town. He's no help neither, which is why I come to you." Lon's words came out measured, slowing as he reached the end, trying to drive his point home.

Martín looked up. "What's your name, mister? Always like to know who I'm talking to."

"Lon Pearce."

The name sparked recognition in the sheriff. He pondered on it a moment. "Name sounds familiar."

"Reckoned it would. 'Fore you go to checking your handbills and finding me in the pile, let me head this off." Lon pulled the document from his shirt and opened it out in front of the lawman. "Amnesty, signed by the governor of New Mexico Territory, all legal and such."

Martín studied the paper. "Hmm. Looks to be in order. How do I know this isn't a forgery?"

"It's real. Send a wire to Governor Wallace to check it out, but we ain't got time to wait on that. Longer this takes, more them folks're in danger."

The sheriff raised his gaze to his visitor. "All right, I'll assume for the time being this is real. How'd you come by your information about the mine anyway?"

"I's part of the slave gang till I got shed a the place."

"Well, good for you. Why didn't you just keep on going?"

Lon hit the desk with his fist. "Damn it, he's got my wife. She's still there."

The sheriff sat back, nodding. "Now we're getting somewhere."

Lon showed his impatience. "'Bout damn time."

Martín leaned forward, angered. "Look, Pearce, you came to me, not the other way around. You can't blame me for being careful committing maybe a dozen men to something I have no knowledge of."

"I get that, Sheriff, but every minute passes, my wife is still stuck there and maybe somebody else dies."

"Hold on. Somebody died?"

"Yeah, they done already killed one fellow, was kinda feeble, not up to working. Just keeled over. I'm trying to keep that from happening again, maybe to my wife this time."

"Look, I never said I wouldn't help you, but I need chapter and verse on this so I know what we're in for."

Frustrated, Lon turned in a complete circle, his hand at the back of his neck. He raised his voice. "We ain't got time to talk this out. I'll tell you what you need to know once we get to riding."

Martín came to his feet, pointing a finger at Lon. "Now, you listen to me. I'm the sheriff here—"

"Yeah, well, you ain't doing much of a job at it you ask me."

Martín fumed. "I'm not asking you." He hesitated, calming himself. "You want my help, you tell it full out right now, or you get the hell out of my office. What's it going to be?"

Lon took a second to cool down. He was boxed into the long way around this, but he needed to relate the most abbreviated version he could think of. He spoke fast, covering everything from the first encounter with the outlaws to his fruitless efforts in Colinas de Oro. The sheriff listened intently, changing his disposition from anger to concern as Lon progressed.

"Now, that's better. You'll get your posse. It'll take me a while to raise 'em. You'll need to be ready to ride by then."

"I'm ready now, Sheriff."

While the sheriff formed a posse, Lon took the time to care for Gray and to consume a meal to replenish his strength. At a window seat in the café across from the sheriff's office, he watched Martín dart around to several buildings in the vicinity, then saw people flooding into the street, heading for the livery. The sheriff spoke to several bystanders, motivating them to action as well.

He had to eat to keep up his strength, but his heart wasn't in it as he poked at his food. Constantly in the back of his mind was his concern for Rhiann. Until now, he'd never had to deal with the desperation of saving a loved one, save for the incidents involving his parents, and that was in the distant past. He stared out the window at the activity in the street as citizens assembled to participate in the posse. He struggled to keep his fear for Rhiann at bay, to prevent it from distracting him from the mission.

Astride Gray, he returned to the sheriff's office to find a group of variously outfitted riders, numbering about a dozen, waiting in the street outside. Lon approached as Martín exited the office carrying a carbine. He seated the gun in its saddle scabbard and mounted his waiting horse. Lon came alongside him.

"Fill us in, Pearce. What are we riding into?"

Lon spoke up to be heard by each member. "We're looking at half a dozen gun sharks, maybe more by now. I've dealt with one of 'em before. He's a mean one. His *compadres*'re no better."

"All right. We're not bulling in there flat out, guns-a-blazing. I'll assess it on the scene and plan it out from there."

"Whatever you say, Sheriff. Shit, can we just go?"

The sheriff took the lead, flanked by Lon. The posse followed at a lope as they set out northwest.

———

GRACE APPLIED A COOL WET cloth to Rhiann's face where Garand's hand had swatted her. A red welt was evident now. Grace sought to allay the pain and to minimize the effect. They spoke in hushed tones to prevent Rita, standing nearby, from overhearing.

"You could have gotten yourself killed."

"Or I could have gotten us out of this. I waited too long though. I should have turned that gun on Garand immediately when I had surprise on my side. That could have given us the advantage."

"Would you have killed him?" Grace seemed put off by the prospect.

"If need be. We've got to fight him on his level."

"Rhiann, nothing can justify killing anyone."

"I agree with that in principle, but practically, this comes down to kill or be killed. I need to know I can depend on you to back me if it comes to it."

Grace took the compress from Rhiann's face and checked the results. "I'll do what I can, but I can't condone killing. I think if you get a chance to get away from this alone, you should take it."

Rhiann shook her head. "I am *not* going to leave you and Mildred behind."

"You might not have that choice."

Rita came closer, speaking as she approached. "All right, ladies, enough of this touchy-feely chit-chat. Get back to work." She shoved Rhiann's shoulder.

Rhiann caught herself on the table to prevent a fall.

Mildred shrank back, while Grace stood flat-footed.

Rhiann pushed off from the table, turning to confront Rita. "Back off, bitch!"

Rita stopped short, glaring at Rhiann. "You watch your step, lady. You heard Victor. He'll kill you next time you step outta line."

"And I'm sure you'll run to tell him all about it, won't you? 'Cause you're in so tight with him, right? You're the one who better watch your step, Rita. He'll toss you aside like an old shirt when he's done with you. Then you'll end up like the rest of us."

Angered, Rita growled, "You little—" Her hands darted toward Rhiann's throat. Rhiann swung her arm up to smack Rita's hands away as she landed the heel of an open hand on Rita's upper chest, shoving her back and upsetting her balance. Wide open, Rita had no defense as Rhiann hunched and lunged forward using her shoulder to batter Rita in the chest. The blow lifted Rita off her feet and dropped her heavily on her back, knocking the wind out of her.

Rhiann straddled the woman and pinned her to the floor with her knees. She used her arm to apply pressure to Rita's throat, cutting her breath, eliciting a low gurgle. "Time you learned I'm not fooling. Now, you're going to listen to me or you're done breathing. Get it?" She kept a steady force on Rita's windpipe until Rita managed to nod agreement.

Rhiann relaxed the hold but kept the hand in place, ready to resume. Rita sucked in a loud breath and coughed. Then slowly her breathing returned to normal. Rhiann kept her pinned to the floor.

"What the hell do you think you're accomplishing, taking up with him?" She quelled more of Rita's struggles. "What do you do, Rita...? What do you do... when he's tired of you?"

Rita flailed her head from side to side. Rhiann, unsure of the woman's intention, pushed on. "You'll have no friends here. You'll be all alone… no help, no support."

Grace joined Rhiann, taking a knee beside her and leaning in toward Rita. "She's right, Rita. You'll never make it alone. None of us will. We've got to stick together to get through this alive."

Then Mildred came to Rhiann's other side in a crouch. "Rita, please. We have to get away from here. I can't take any more of this." She was almost in tears.

Rita turned her head away in silence.

Rhiann drove it on. "Something else to consider. He put you in charge of us, didn't he? What happens when he finds out you're on the receiving end of this… this… revolt? And he will find out. I'll see to that. Think your life'll be worth anything then?"

Grace leaned in closer. "Listen to reason, Rita. All our lives are in the balance here."

Rita shook her head, leading Rhiann to wonder if she was refusing or trying to squirm out of her grip. "What do you say, Rita? You ready to work *with* us?"

Rita seemed to drift off in her reverie. Her voice was gruff from being throttled, coming out in a whisper that might have been unintentional. "I thought I was protecting myself, the only way I know how." A look of disgust crossed her face. Her voice rose to a coarse shout. "Uhnh! He disgusts me. I been with a lot a shitty characters, but he's the worst. I can't stand him."

Rhiann retained her hold on Rita's throat. "Then don't make it for naught. Put it to good use. The more we know about Garand, the more we can use against him. It might get us what we need to escape. Then we can bring back help and put an end to this."

Rita considered for a long moment, then nodded. "Yeah, all right, I'll help."

Rhiann floated off into her own daydream as thoughts of Lon and what he might be up to took her over. Rita's scratchy voice jolted her back to reality. "I said I'd help. You going to let me up or what?"

Rhiann let go of Rita's throat, hauled herself up, and stepped away. Grace and Mildred helped Rita to her feet. She pushed at their hands, turned away, and sat on her cot to regain herself.

Grace moved close to Rhiann to whisper. "Do you think we can trust her?"

Rhiann shook her head but did not answer. True, she had no choice but to work with Rita. It was a start, but trust was something else. She'd have to keep a close eye on the woman.

17

IT WAS LATE AFTERNOON OF their second day out. Riding a few paces ahead of the posse, Lon, trailed closely by the sheriff, recognized the terrain they had entered a few miles back. It was the same rocky country he'd covered on his escape from the mine.

He pulled Gray up, raising his hand to halt the group. Martín came alongside.

Lon pointed ahead. "We're close. Mine's yonder a that rise, maybe half a mile or so."

"Then we'll hold 'em up here. You and I will go in closer and have a look around. I'll figure it out from there."

Lon nodded. He and Martín dismounted. The sheriff signaled the others to get down and gather around. He spoke to the group in a low voice.

"Hold up here. Take a breather. No noise, no fires. Pearce and I're going in for a look-see. Wait here for us."

Lon ground tied Gray. "Mounts're too easy to spot. Best we go in on foot."

Lon and Martín left the group and walked the few hundred yards to the rise, then ascended the grade, keeping a low profile upon reaching the crest. The terrain straightened to level ground before blending into a higher slope.

"Far side a that hill leads down into a canyon. Mine's in there. Keep low."

Trees and random boulders dotted the landscape, offering them concealment. Without that, lookouts could spot them easily.

Lon stopped and spoke in a whisper. "Stay close. Follow what I do." He led a strategic pattern, darting from tree to boulder to maintain camouflage. Martín mimicked him, staying close.

Half way across the flats, the sheriff raised a halting hand. They crouched behind a boulder to take a breather.

"Guess I've had too much desk duty." He took a deep breath. "I'm curious. How'd you come by that amnesty paper?"

"Did a job a work for the governor."

"Must have been pretty important to warrant him issuing that."

"He thought as much."

Martín leaned closer. "Just so you know, I don't trust any outlaw, amnesty or not."

"Yeah, well, just so *you* know, feeling's mutual." Lon took a beat to let that sink in. "You 'bout blowed out?"

"I guess."

Keeping close watch on the ridge, Lon led out toward the base of the slope with the sheriff at his heels. They continued an erratic pattern until they reached the grade, a forty-five-degree angle of rocky, uneven ground. They crouched at the base to confer.

"It's right over that ridge. Keep low."

The sheriff nodded.

They set out in a hunkered-down advance that transitioned into a low crawl about a quarter of the way from the crest. Removing their hats to lower their profiles, they elbowed their way to a vantage point high above the mine. Martín took his first look as Lon outlined the operation in a whisper, then continued to the important details. "They keep my wife and the other women in that small cabin they use as a cook shack. The men get bedded down in the open. The guards're in the cabin near the corral. They was usual keeping the grounds covered by one guard at night. That might a changed since I got loose. Reckon they'd a figured I'd be back."

The sheriff scanned the scene once more. "I don't like operating in the dark. Too chancy. We can move in at daybreak, surround 'em, take 'em by surprise."

"Suit yourself, but Rawls and his gunnies, they ain't rolling over peaceable-like. It ain't right them women being in the middle a that shit, day or night. I'll go in tonight, get 'em out. Once they're safe, you can run it anyway you want."

"You're just bound and determined to take chances, aren't you?"

Lon had enough of this pretender. "And you're just bound and determined to play it safe, ain't you? 'Bout time you do what the hell they pay you to do."

"Who the hell you think you are, telling me how to run my office? You got any idea how hard it is for an *hombre* with my background, a name like Alejandro Martín, to gain the respect this badge represents? I've worked hard to get here. I'm not doing anything to put that in jeopardy. Nothing."

And there it was, the thing sticking in Martín's craw. It didn't phase Lon in the least. "Sheriff, I don't much care what you been through or where you trying to get to. We all of us got our pasts coming back to haunt us. It ain't what you come from, it's what you do matters. Time you quit hiding behind your past and do your job."

Martín took a long pause. He shook his head. "Son of a bitch. I'm not debating this with you. I'll be damned if I sit still and let a known goddam outlaw preach down to me."

Lon shot back. "Yeah, well, to my mind, you might could do a lot worse. Now, look, I'm going in after the women. Tonight. I get them out, the rest of it's yours, and I'll side you in it anyways you want."

"How the hell you think you can pull this off without rousting that whole camp?"

"I stayed a jump ahead a the law better'n fifteen years. I can move like a snake when I need to. And my wife's been down a trail or two herself. Worked with the Pinkertons. We'll get it handled, no frets."

Martín's hand grabbed Lon's shoulder. "Fair warning, Pearce—this backfires, I'll have your ass in a cell for obstructing, quicker'n you can—"

"Sheriff, this backfires, I doubt I'll be alive to worry about a cell. Now, you 'bout ready to head back?"

Martín seemed resigned to the situation, but his reply was more of a grunt. "Yeah."

LON BIDED HIS TIME, THANKFUL as darkness blanketed the area that he had the light of a full moon to help him make his way. The sheriff had already settled his posse into a cold camp to await the results of Lon's foray into the mine complex. Waiting until he was sure the workers and the guards had retired for the night, Lon left the group on foot and headed toward the vantage point on the ridge. Moving forward carefully, the bright moonlight perfectly outlined a rifleman on the slope near the top of the ridge. It would have been easy to skirt around the guard without detection, but that left open the possibility of the man stopping him and the women on their way back to the posse. The threat had to be dealt with now.

Ducking behind a large bush, he settled on a distraction to take the man unaware. He felt around on the ground for a stone large enough to make sufficient noise to attract the guard's attention. A toss to his left produced the desired results as the stone slashed its way noisily through thick bushes.

As the rifleman moved forward to investigate, Lon watched from hiding, ready to strike. The man stopped for a look, his back to Lon's position. Maintaining silence, Lon moved in behind the guard, drawing his revolver. Impulse caused the man to start turning, sensing something behind him, but Lon's gun barrel landed hard on the side of his head before he could finish the move. The man grunted and went limp, collapsing to the ground. Lon crouched, ready to continue the attack, but it was clear the man was unconscious. He pulled the man's iron and, extracting the cylinder pin, he disassembled the weapon, and tossed the components into various spots in the bushes, followed by the rifle. The rustling sounds made by the weapons gave Lon pause to check if he had attracted further attention. His few seconds of hesitation resulted in silence. He looked at the guard again, willing him to stay unconscious, then continued up the slope, keeping to a low crawl.

At the crest, on his belly, Lon scanned the area below. The abundant moonlight afforded sharp images, revealing the presence of a guard seated in front of the smelting equipment across from the kitchen. His next step was to clear a path to the kitchen for access to the women. The same light source that had played to his advantage now threatened to hinder his movements and reveal his presence. This would take some ciphering.

He stayed in the prone position for the next few minutes, racking his brain for a plan and coming up empty. There had to be a way. The distance to the kitchen was too great to bridge in the moonlight without attracting the guard unless he was asleep. But he was wide awake and alert. Lon waited.

After a few tense moments, the guard rose and walked across the yard between the kitchen building and Garand's cabin. The outhouse was back there. The guard likely had the urge. Lon calculated his chances of reaching the outhouse before the guard finished and emerged. They were pretty slim, considering the distance, but this was his only chance. He'd have to make it work or risk the possibility of rousing the camp.

Waiting until the guard had disappeared behind the kitchen, Lon scrambled to his feet and followed an erratic pattern down the slope into the yard. He stumbled on an ill-placed stone, tripped, and fell, rolling the final few feet to the base of the hill. He stayed down, scanning the area where the prisoners slept. No one stirred. Regaining his footing on level ground, he continued at a dead run between the corral and the guards' quarters. Running along the base of the opposite slope, past the shack, he rounded the back of the outhouse as he heard movement inside. Stopping at the front corner of the hut, he waited for the door to open as he tried to catch his wind.

He peered around the corner as the door opened, then ducked back. The increased odor from the outhouse hit Lon in the face as Hatcher stepped out hitching his pants, his Sharps rifle balanced in the crook of his arm. Lon's thought as he moved behind Hatcher and drew his sidearm, was that he'd almost caught the man with his pants down. A wide swing brought the weapon across the back of Hatcher's head with a dull crack that seemed louder than it was in the quiet of the night. Hatcher winced and pitched forward, falling in a clump at Lon's feet. He appeared to rally for a second, tensing Lon to prepare for further action, but then he stopped moving. Lon grabbed the rifle from the ground and tossed it into the bushes behind the hut, then hauled Hatcher's limp body into the building to lay him on the floor. Stepping out, he closed the door and headed for the kitchen.

At the kitchen's back door, he paused to glance around, making certain no other obstacles existed. Shielded by the structure from the moon's direct light back here, he felt around for the latch. His hand brushed a piece of wood inserted between the door and the jamb, likely a wedge to keep the door from being opened from inside. He gripped it and worked it loose. Discarding the wedge, he opened the door quietly and stepped inside. He stopped to give his eyes a moment to adjust to the increased darkness of the room, lighted only by moonlight drifting in from one slightly open window. Immediately, the relaxed, measured breathing of the sleeping women became audible to him.

As his eyes let in more of the images before him, he made out the outline of Rhiann's features on one of the cots. He'd viewed that profile on many a moonlit night as she slept in several of their camps during the journey north. No mistaking that face, even in this low light.

He moved gingerly to the cot, crouched, and laid his hand gently over her mouth. Leaning in, he whispered her name in her ear. She stirred and opened her eyes, startled.

He spoke in a hushed tone. "Shhh, it's me." He lifted his hand from her mouth.

Rhiann was instantly awake and alert. "What're you doing here?" She seemed in disbelief.

"Getting you out a here. Wake the others. We got to go."

Working methodically, Rhiann got into her boots and moved first to Grace's bunk where she gently awakened the woman and whispered to her. "Lon's here. We need to go now."

Grace nodded, throwing back her blanket and pulling on shoes. "Get Rita."

Grace moved to Rita's bunk to find the blond already popping up, reaching for her shoes, as Rhiann leaned over Mildred and placed a quieting hand over the girl's mouth. "Mildred." She came awake abruptly, making a grunt. "Shh! We're getting out of here. Don't make a sound."

Mildred nodded understanding. Rhiann removed her hand and helped her up. Rhiann helped her on with her shoes. They moved to join Lon and the other women coming together at the back door.

Mildred, as she passed the prep table, tripped on her skirts. Her grab for support moved the table, causing its legs to scrape the floor in a noisy squawk. Everything stopped dead. Rhiann, behind her, grabbed her arm at the elbow and helped her to maintain her position as Mildred shot an embarrassed look over her shoulder. Rhiann ushered her to the others.

Lon listened through the door for a second, then spoke in a hushed tone. "I took care a the guard. We get outside, head for the corral, then across to the south hill. They's a path up and over it. I'll show you. Posse's waiting half a mile straight yonder a that. Don't stop, not for nothing, till you reach 'em, savvy?"

Anxiously, they nodded their understanding. Filing out, they moved quickly along the buildings. Lon led them behind the corral and raised a hand to halt them. The horses and the fences helped to conceal them. He pointed across the yard.

"That's the path there. Head for it and keep going, no matter what. I'll hang back, make sure you ain't followed."

Rhiann hesitated, grabbing Lon's arm. "No, you—"

Lon pulled free. "Don't wait for me, I'll catch up. Go."

With Rhiann in the lead, the women crossed the yard quickly and started up the path. Lon moved to the edge of the corral and crouched for a last scan of the camp. Ready to run, a noise stopped him cold. He looked toward the source, the door to the guards' quarters. He glanced in that direction to see a figure emerge, striking a match on his pants. Lon waited.

The man touched the flame to a smoke and looked around. The match light identified him. Rawls. First noticing the absence of the guard, Rawls scanned the camp as he discarded the match. The sight of the women scrambling up the inclined path put him in motion. Tossing the cigarette, he started in their direction, pulling his sidearm as he moved.

Instantly assessing the situation, Lon stayed behind the corral fence, blending with the milling horses inside. As Rawls passed him, Lon decided against a direct attack. Confronting him here would wake the camp.

As the women disappeared over the ridge, Rawls climbed the path in pursuit. Lon tried to get into Rawls's head. His prior knowledge of the man's way of thinking told him Rawls would pursue the women instead of waking the camp. He'd figure he was more than capable of subduing and recapturing three helpless women on his lonesome. Lon would use that against him.

Running across the yard, Lon began a climb up the rough hill terrain west of the path, staying behind Rawls but keeping the man in sight. Maybe Rawls would be intent enough on catching the women that he wouldn't sense he was being shadowed. Worth a try.

The women continued their ascent until they reached level ground atop the rise. Lon watched them enter a grove of bushes. Rawls hurried to follow them. Cutting across, Lon closed on Rawls. This had to be quick and, this near the camp, quiet as well. He needed to separate Rawls from his gun and take him down.

Rawls moved toward the bushes as Lon came within a few feet of him. Rawls reacted as Lon launched himself at him. As Rawls turned toward the motion, Lon, left hand outstretched, collided with Rawls, gripping Rawls's gun hand as he took the man off his feet. They hit the ground hard, Lon on top in a control position. Instantly, he slammed Rawls's arm against a rock. Rawls let go of the revolver, wincing as his hand hit the stone. Lon's body pinned Rawls's arms and legs to the ground, spread-eagle. Now he had to get him out of reach of the weapon.

Lon grabbed an arm and a handful of shirt to lift Rawls into a roll that would take him away from where the gun lay. Unexpectedly, Rawls helped with that move, pushing with a freed foot in the direction Lon pulled. They rolled several times, fighting for the top position. On the last rotation, Rawls got there, moving to immobilize Lon.

As Rawls moved into position, Lon drew his knee up toward his chest, upsetting Rawls. Shoving his leg out, he caught Rawls in the midsection and pushed him away, then rolled to his feet. Rawls clawed his way to stand as Lon moved in.

Rawls threw an awkward, off-balance swing at Lon's midbody which Lon easily sidestepped, countering with a chop that bounded Rawls back a few steps. Staying on him, Lon advanced, landing two well placed left jabs and a right cross that tore Rawls's head to the side and sent a sharp pain up Lon's arm. Following the momentum his head had begun, Rawls's body spun, landing him on all fours, his back to Lon.

Rawls paused in that position. "Shit!" He spat blood, maybe a tooth, but Lon couldn't tell that for sure.

Holding his fighting position, Lon stood over Rawls. This was odd. Was Rawls just delaying to catch his breath? Lon went along with it, playing for time the women needed to get away clean. He watched Rawls closely, waiting for a movement.

Seconds ticked by, precious seconds Rhiann needed to guide the women to the protection of the posse. Then Rawls moved quickly, rolling to a crouch, reaching along his leg and springing forward. The glint of moonlight on metal gave Lon instant warning. Knife. In his boot. Rawls lunged, the six-inch blade in his outstretch hand aimed for Lon's chest. Lon ducked and dodged as Rawls bounded past him, the thrust narrowly missing him.

Rawls regained his footing and spun around, flipping the knife to hold it for a downward strike. He lunged again. Lon ducked under the man's arm, grabbing the wrist and taking the arm over his shoulder. He added his other hand to the grip. Rawls exerted all his strength trying to plunge the knife home while his free hand clawed at Lon's face, trying to get a grip. Lon evaded the hand, pushed up and back, twisting Rawls's knife arm and forcing the blade back over his shoulder. They struggled in a death lock for several seconds, each trying to exert superior pressure.

With a final effort, Lon pushed on Rawls's wrist to a point at which Rawls had little control. Concentrating his effort, Lon steadily moved the point of the knife closer to Rawls's neck.

Rawls kept trying with his other hand to claw at Lon's face and body, an attempt to inflict pain and weaken Lon's hold on the weapon's path. In response, Lon let go of the knife with his left hand and drove that elbow into Rawls's midsection sharply, diverting Rawls's efforts from pushing on the knife, allowing Lon to redouble the struggle for control of the blade's direction.

Rawls's strength waned. His determination gave over to fear as the blade closed on his neck, causing him to falter. Lon sensed the shift and made one last push, driving the blade home, seating it to the hilt in Rawls's throat. A gurgling sound came from Rawls. Warm blood spurted from the wound onto Lon's back and shoulder as Rawls sagged and relaxed his hold. Lon pushed harder and held the knife in place until Rawls had no more fight left in him. Lon let him go. He collapsed in a heap, the weapon stuck in his throat, his feeble attempts to extract it making no difference. He sprawled out on the ground as death claimed him.

Lon stood there, huffing to get his breath, coming down from the adrenaline rush as he viewed the results of his efforts. It was over. Inhaling a final cleansing breath, it was time to move on, to catch up to the women, to Rhiann, and to rejoin the posse.

The crack of a branch under foot behind him froze him in place as a voice commanded, "You hold it right there!"

18

RHIANN LED THE WOMEN INTO the bushes at the crest of the south hill. They continued moving south through the brush. After emerging onto the flat plain, they hurried across the one-eighth mile expanse. As they crossed, Rhiann, still in the lead, sensed Lon was not behind them. He should have already caught up to them. What happened? She stopped, drawing the attention of the three women. They grouped around her.

Grace voiced the question they all must have had. "Why'd you stop?"

Rhiann looked hard in the direction of the mine, searching for some sign of Lon that she could take as reassurance he was coming. She found none. "Lon should have reached us by now."

"You want to go back and look for him, don't you—?"

Immediately upset, Mildred broke in. "No, no, you can't. You have to stay with us. We don't know what to do without you."

"I'm feeling my way, Mildred, same as you."

"That guy's more than just a friend, ain't he?" Rita asked.

"Yeah. He's my husband."

"Thought so."

Grace came to counsel. "I know you're worried about him, but alone what can you do for him? It's better for us to reach the posse and get their help."

Rhiann took a beat, then nodded. "Yeah, you're right. Come on, keep going."

They pressed on in search of the posse, continuing over the bright moonlit flats. At several points, Mildred stumbled. Grace came to her aid each time, grabbing her by the shoulders or the waist to help her up and to stabilize her.

Exhausted, Mildred tripped and fell to her knees. She stayed in that position supported by her hands, staring at the ground. "I can't… I can't do this."

Grace crouched beside her. "It's only a little way on, Mildred. You can make it. We'll help you." She lifted the girl to her feet. Rhiann came to her other side. She and Grace each put one of her arms over their shoulders to support her. They moved on, Rita bringing up the rear, glancing over her shoulder to spot followers.

A little over three hundred yards brought them to the top of the ridge below which the posse was grouped together.

Rhiann saw them first. "There they are. Come on." Wearily, they descended the slope into the midst of the group. As the men crowded around, a man with a sheriff's badge stepped forward.

"Ladies, are you all right?"

"Exhausted," was Rhiann's reply. "But all right for the most part."

Grace assumed the burden of holding Mildred as Rhiann ducked under the girl's arm and moved closer to the sheriff.

Martín gazed at her. "I'm Sheriff Martín, ma'am. That's a nasty bruise you got there."

"Could've been worse. We need to go back and find my husband."

"Your husband?"

"Yes, my husband, Lon Pearce. He got us out and stayed back to cover our escape, but he never caught up to us. I think he's in trouble."

The sheriff gave a knowing nod. "Yeah, maybe, but I'm not moving these men till daylight. Too dangerous in the dark."

Rhiann was aghast. "Lon could be dead by morning."

"Ma'am, your husband knew what he was getting into when he talked me into letting him go in alone. I can't risk the lives of these men to pull his irons out of a fire he caused for himself. Sorry. We don't move till first light."

Frustrated, Rhiann glared at the uncooperative lawman. The expression on his face told her he was resolute. Further arguments would be fruitless and a waste of precious time. Instead, she shot him a glare that could have singed his skin as her mind put together a hasty strategy. She looked past him to the remuda grazing nearby, singling out Gray, saddled and ready to go. Pushing her way through the posse members, she strode defiantly toward Gray.

"Ma'am." The sheriff's summons went unheeded as Rhiann reached Gray and stroked the horse's neck and muzzle. Gathering Gray's reins, she swung into the saddle and urged the big animal forward. "Let's go find Lon, boy." The horse seemed to understand her words, moving with determination.

As they picked up speed to ride past the group, Sheriff Martín stepped out from the crowd and stood directly in their path, his hands raised in a stop signal. Rhiann pulled Gray up at the last second.

"Can't let you do this, ma'am." He reached out to grab Gray's halter. The horse reared and backed off.

"You got no say in this. Step aside or we'll run you down."

Gray reared again, with less height this time.

"Ma'am, I—"

"Try arguing with this horse, you'll lose. Now get out of the way." She dug her heels into Gray's flanks as the sheriff reluctantly did her bidding, bounding to the side on unsteady legs. Gray continued forward, reaching a gallop at the base of the rise and taking the ridge in a few vaults.

LON FROZE AS FOLEY'S SHARP voice behind him stopped him. He read the threat in the words. There had to be a revolver backing it up. Caught flat footed, Lon stayed put, waiting for an opening. Foley's footsteps got louder as he approached.

"You hold right still there."

Lon sensed the man moving in an arc behind him to get a closer look at the body on the ground. Foley came into his peripheral vision as he moved in to stoop over Rawls.

"That's Rawls. You son-of-a-bitch, you done killed Rawls."

Gleaning Foley's upset over the loss of his friend, Lon upped the tension, trying to rile him into making a mistake. "Damn right. Got what was coming to him."

"Got him in the back, eh? Bastard."

Lon stayed on it. "I got him looking. Right up front."

Foley fumed, stepping in close. "I ought a drop you right here, goddamn it."

Lon stood his ground. "Come on, or you as yellow as him?"

That tore it. Foley raised the gun over his head, intending to strike—the mistake Lon sought. He moved quicker, throwing up a hand to block the gun's arc and another to shove a fist into his chest. Pushed back, Foley stumbled, tripped over Rawls's body and caught himself before he fell over. The gun out of play for a second, Lon dove for the bushes as his hand fetched the Colt from his holster. Branches and vines brushed his body as he plummeted into them and disappeared from Foley's view. Landing on his side, he rolled to a sitting position, sighting through the obstructions as Foley could be heard regaining his footing and crunching into the brush.

Others joined Foley. Lon heard multiple footsteps and familiar voices as Snake and Red crowded in. Thinking better of giving away his position and alerting the camp by firing, Lon moved as quietly as possible toward the flats beyond the bushes. If he could make it through, a dead run might put him close enough to the posse's location to draw these *hombres* into a trap. His best chance for survival. He stayed low and kept moving.

The absence of sounds behind him indicated his pursuers were not near. The flats were within reach. He emerged and holstered his weapon, intending to launch into a mad run.

"Hey, *amigo, manos arriba, eh?*" Paco's voice split the night silence.

Lon glanced to his right. The Mexican, a *cigarillo* dangling from his mouth, stood nonchalantly, the barrel of his revolver moving in a slight upward arc to illustrate his order. Then it settled on Lon's middle. At this range, he couldn't miss if he tried. Lon chose the only option, raising his hands to shoulder level.

Paco advanced and placed his gun barrel inches from Lon's face as he reached the Colt from Lon's hand, staring ominously into Lon's eyes. He stepped back, shoving the iron in his waist band. "Hey, *amigos,* over here." His call was loud enough to wake the dead.

Out of chances, Lon stood his ground as footfalls sounded through the brush, smashing bushes and twigs. Foley came out first, moved to Lon, and landed a right hook on Lon's jaw, reeling him back. He stayed on his feet as the others crowded around. Surrounded, Lon could do no more than rub the spot where the fist had connected. His dignity took more of a wound than the puny blow had inflicted.

Paco's smoke wobbled in his mouth as he spoke. "What we do with him?"

Foley thought for a second. "We ought a just put his lights out permanent for doing Rawls like he done, but naw, we'll take him to Garand. He'll want to have his fun."

Paco again presented his revolver in Lon's face. "Let's walk, eh?"

Lon glared at the man.

The others closed around him and steered him the long way around the bushes toward the camp's south hill. In the middle, with four guns on him, he cooperated to avoid reprisals he knew were just waiting to be delivered.

Cresting the hill, they started down the slope as activity in the no longer sleeping camp increased. Drawden and Lakota had assumed guard duty, standing at strategic points on the yard. Hatcher, clutching the Sharps, entered the yard from between the kitchen and Garand's cabin, holding his head. They all came together in the center of the yard, Lon now covered by every gun.

Foley sniffed at Hatcher. "You smell worse'n usual."

"Aw, shut up."

Lon almost cracked a smile at that but thought better of it.

The door to the cabin opened. Garand stepped out, slipping suspenders over his shoulders. He approached the group. "What's going on?" He made no secret of his displeasure at being turned out in the middle of the night. "What the hell's all this?"

Foley stepped out to meet him. "Pearce done Rawls in. We brung him back for you."

Curiosity on Garand's face became anger. He moved close to Lon. "You're not going to like the consequences this brings you. One thing puzzles me though. You were clear of this place. What made you come back?"

Lon simply stared at Garand, not answering.

Garand pondered for a long moment. "There's more to this." He looked to Foley. "Roust everyone. Get them all out here."

Foley moved quickly, rounding up the randomly placed workers and herding them into a tight group near Lon and Garand. As they crowded around, several of the guards took up strategic positions to contain them. Foley crossed to the kitchen and stepped inside. In a second, he bounded back out. "The womens gone."

Garand returned his attention to Lon, nodding knowingly. "And that's it. You came back for the women. I knew there was more between you and that Rhiann than you let on. Where are they?"

Lon stood silent.

Garand backhanded him a slap that tore his head to the side and opened a trail of blood at the corner of his mouth. "Answer me. Where are they?"

Lon recovered to stand straight, glaring at Garand. "Where you can't touch 'em no more."

Seething, Garand turned and took a few steps away, his hand rubbing his chin in thought. "More consequences." His voice was barely audible. Then he faced Lon. "Give me a gun." His hand went out, palm up, waiting to be filled.

Snake, standing closest, turned his revolver around and laid the butt in Garand's hand. Garand cocked the piece and fired off-handed without aiming. The slug creased Lon's upper left arm, slashing a cut into his flesh just above the scar of a previous wound. Instinctively, Lon's right hand went to the spot, gripping just below the rip in his shirt sleeve as pain shot through his arm, and blood ran into the garment.

A smile of pleasure crossed Garand's face. "Just a taste...." He let that trail off.

Lon's glare remained insolent.

Garand met his stare and spoke to the group without facing them, concentrating on Lon. "Now listen to me, all of you. You're about to see what happens to one who crosses me. And you'd better learn from this because the same will happen to any one of you with similar intentions. Stand back. Give me room. This will not be quick, but I promise you it will definitely be painful."

The guards moved the workers back a few feet, grouping them together tightly in front of the kitchen building, covering them from all sides. Garand and Lon were left facing each other alone in the center of the yard.

Lon's mind raced to find a way out before Garand finished grandstanding and actually got to doing what was on his mind. He came up with nothing but the possibility of attacking Garand before he could fire and using him as a shield. That would not end well, but at least he'd put up a fight before going down. He tensed as Garand took a few steps back and slowly aimed the weapon.

The sound in the distance caught Lon's attention first. Garand seemed engrossed in his need to draw this out and to make his example to the prisoners. He either failed to hear it, or he disregarded it. Definitely hoof beats. One horse. Coming in from the approach road. Coming in fast.

Lon glanced quickly to his right but found it hard to believe what he saw. Gray, plain as day in the moonlight, with Rhiann in the saddle, running flat out for them. His gaze returned to Garand, who still did not acknowledge the approach. What was Rhiann doing? Best to hold Garand's attention on himself away from Rhiann and Gray. He groaned aloud, glancing at the wound. "Shit! That hurts. What the hell you waiting for?"

"I'm enjoying this, or—" Then, too late, he caught on. His head turned slightly, but by then, they were on him.

Rhiann shouted at Gray, urging the horse on, directly in Garand's path. Guards and prisoners alike stood transfixed. Garand's inadequate reaction couldn't prevent the collision as Gray's hooves reached him, knocking him aside. The horse kept going as Garand's body tumbled to the side. Lon watched him hit the ground hard, losing the gun. Rhiann pulled hard rein. Gray skidded to a stop and spun around, looking ready for another run at the man.

Dumbfounded, the guards focused on Garand as he rolled to a stop six feet away. With random precision and abandon, the prisoners rallied, grabbed at the guards, pushing, pulling, knocking them over, pouncing several at a time on them. Random shots went wild as hands grabbed at weapons, wrenching them away. Taken to the ground by men piling on them, the guards were pummeled into submission by fists and feet.

Foley lost his sidearm as Strome and Flick, working together, tripped him and pounced on him. Paco and the others found themselves in a similar predicament. Snake's whip was ripped from his hand. Still coiled, the lash was used as a club on his face and head. Shouts and screams fueled the rebellion. It happened so quickly, so intensely, that the guards had no chance to fight back. They were separated from their weapons, pinned in place by knees, hands, anything available.

Lon saw his Colt taken from Paco and tossed aside. He hurried to retrieve it.

Rhiann trotted Gray back to where Lon stood. "Lon—"

Seeing her focus on his wounded arm, he sought to reassure her. "I'm all right."

She slid out of the saddle and ran to him. He hurried to place his gun in the saddlebag before he scooped her into his arms in a bear hug that was overdue for both of them. "You took a hell of a chance there."

She nuzzled into him, giving a nervous giggle. "You're worth it." She stepped back. "Your arm—"

Lon shook his head. "Just a scratch. Had worse."

She pulled the bandana from her neck and wrapped it around his arm to cover the opening in a makeshift bandage. Then she stepped back to give him a view of the conquest taking place. Insurgent prisoners leaned on, sat on guards, pinning them in place.

As Lon and Rhiann started toward the crowd, his protective arm around her, another sound reached their ears. They glanced at its source, the south hill, as posse members scaled the slope and entered the yard, guns drawn. A few others descended the north slope to join them. Sheriff Martín in the lead, they came to a halt in the center of the yard and dismounted. The sheriff approached, scanning the scene. He seemed to understand what had occurred.

Lon spoke as the lawman reached them. "Reckon they handled it."

Martín looked around again. "So I see. You know, wasn't for your wife, we'd a waited till daybreak, but she forced my hand. Couldn't let her ride in here alone. She could a got herself killed."

Rhiann answered up. "And Lon'd be dead if I'd waited. No thanks to you."

Lon flashed a grin. "Reckon you don't know Rhiann all that well. She sets her mind to something, you ain't changing it. She gets it done her way."

"Mighty well told." Martín eyed Lon's arm. "That need tending?"

Lon shook his head. Rhiann gripped him tighter.

The sheriff looked around at the scene. "We took out a few guards up on the ridges. Looks like all we got to do here is mop up the rest a these knotheads."

Lon nodded. "Them… and him." He indicated the spot where Garand had landed, the spot now conspicuously vacant.

19

O N THE PERIPHERY OF THE melee in progress in the middle of the yard as prisoners vented their wrath on the guards, Garand lay stunned on his side in the spot he'd rolled to after being pummeled by that savage of a horse. Dizzy, but still aware of the scene before him, he hurt in several places where hooves had contacted flesh and bone. A quick assessment told him nothing was broken. He was intact, if somewhat the worse for wear. *The gun!* Where was the gun? Without moving, he glanced around, spotting the weapon on the ground not three feet from where he'd landed. Careful to maintain his low profile, he scrambled closer, reached out, and grabbed the thing.

Switching his gaze to the activity in front of him, it was clear his minions were outnumbered and in the process of being neutralized. It was only a matter of minutes before he'd be noticed, and would suffer the same fate. *Move! Get out of there!*

A panicked glance gave him direction. The cook shack was right there. All he had to do was get behind it for an initial hiding place. Holding the revolver, he low-crawled toward the side of the building, then glanced back. No one reacted to his move. He continued.

Painful seconds later, he reached the rear of the structure and allowed it to swallow his form. Only when he was sure no one had noticed his exit did he move farther. By now, the dizziness had dissipated some. Conscious enough, he assessed his options, settling on use of that little alcove in the mineshaft that would completely hide him from general view. Even someone on a mission to locate him would find it difficult, if not impossible. He made for it.

Moving with stealth, he darted painfully along the rear of the shack, bridging the gap between it and the cabin, then behind the cabin, and, hugging the rock wall at the end of the canyon, made his way to the shaft opening. Another quick glance at the confusion in the yard told him he was still safe from view, though he wasn't sure why since he was right out in the open. No matter. He slipped into the mine.

Six feet in, what little moonlight had penetrated the shaft petered out. Feeling his way in the dark along the wall, he advanced another twelve or so feet. There his hand lost purchase on the wall. That was his goal. The little depression in the shaft he'd noticed several weeks earlier, into which he could sink, would hide him from a search. He ducked into it, hunkering down to lick his wounds and wait this out. The sounds of the activity in the yard seemed a bit distant but were audible to him. This would allow him to monitor the situation and decide when venturing out would be safe. It might even give him the opportunity to vent his wrath on Pearce and that woman of his. If that became possible, he had degradations in mind for them before they died slowly at his hand. All he had to do was stay put and listen. His time would come, as would theirs.

"WHO? THE SHERIFF STARED AT the section of ground Lon pointed to, no longer bearing Garand's battered form.

"Garand. The *hombre* running this fiasco. Gray roughed him up a mite. That's where he landed. The hell'd he get to?"

"Maybe crawled off in the confusion." Martín turned to his posse, assembled near the horses. "Couple a you fellows take a look around. We got one of these jokers missing."

Several posse members went to work searching the area. After a less than thorough examination, they came up empty. Even a cursory check inside the mineshaft, using a lantern, turned up nothing.

The sheriff was not dismayed. "He can't get far on foot. We'll run him down in the morning. Right now, I need to sort this mess out."

"That's easy." Lon pointed to the struggle around them. "The ones pinned down're the ones you want to lock up. Rest of 'em the ones done your job for you."

Martín flashed a scowl at Lon for the dig. He started toward the group of liberated prisoners and their captives, leaving Lon and Rhiann holding each other in the center of the yard.

Rhiann spoke quietly to Lon. "Shouldn't we go after Garand?"

"Ain't our problem." He tossed his head in the sheriff's direction. "It's his. We're done with it, and good riddance."

They watched as the sheriff walked into the aftermath of the melee, checking wounds, examining unconscious forms. There was a lot of blood on both sides, but no fatalities. Outnumbered, the outlaws had fought, then tried to run, but determined townsmen took them down and dealt an overabundance of retaliation. Martín spoke to a few residents he seemed familiar with, then he spotted and singled out Strome. "The hell're you doing here?"

Strome tried to look in charge, failing at it. "Flick and me were up here searching for Garand after he escaped. We got caught when him and his men attacked. They killed my jailer. Worked him to death."

A voice from the group spoke up. "That ain't how it happened, Sheriff." The voice's owner stepped in close to the sheriff and whispered in his ear for a long moment. When the man finished, he stepped back. Martín went face to face with Strome.

"What I'm hearing is you and the assayer jumped this claim out from under Garand. That right?"

"Naw, Sheriff, it ain't like that."

Flick stepped up to inject himself into the confrontation. "Garand never filed his claim. He killed his partner and escaped. Claim was up for grabs."

"And you two made damn sure you grabbed it." Martín glanced over his shoulder. "Pearce. You got anything to add here?"

Lon nodded. "Way I heard it, Flick set Garand up. Then they railroaded him so they could file on it. Now they trying to lie their way out of it."

The sheriff turned his attention back to Strome and Flick, addressing Strome. "I'll take your gun and that badge. We'll figure this out back in Ironsight."

"Aw, Sheriff, you ain't going to—"

"You heard me, Strome. Hand 'em over." Martín glared at Flick. "And you, shut the hell up."

Reluctantly, they complied.

Martín handed the weapons off to a deputy. "Take these two in with the others. Lock 'em up."

A posse member called out a warning. "Rider coming."

The sheriff looked to where the man pointed. A horseman, at a furious pace, rode down the south slope. Martín seemed a bit overwhelmed. "Now what?"

The rider came straight at them at a gallop and pulled up short as the sheriff approach him. "Sheriff." The man's breath was short. "One of them women's gone."

"What do you mean gone? Gone where?"

"I don't know. She run off when I wasn't looking. No idea where."

"Which one?"

"That young one, the jittery one."

Listening to the conversation, Rhiann spoke quietly. "Mildred."

Martín shot his deputy a look of disappointment. "Damn, Des, you said you could handle it."

"I'm sorry, Sheriff. She's gone 'fore I knowed it. No sign a where."

"What about the other two?"

"Still at camp."

"All right, get on back to them. No sense trying to track in the dark. We'll look for the missing one in the morning."

The man turned his horse and set out to retrace his tracks, climbing the hill and disappearing over the ridge.

Martín went back to where Lon and Rhiann stood.

Rhiann pressed him. "You'll find her, won't you?"

"Oh, we'll find her all right. How far can one greenhorn gal get on foot?"

"She doesn't want to go back to her husband. She says he beats her."

The sheriff seemed fed up with constant developments. "Huh! Well, she's going to have to work that out with him. He's her legal guardian. Law says I got to take her back to him."

"Sheriff—"

Martín raised a halting hand. "Ma'am, this is not up for discussion. The law is clear on this. I got to do what the law dictates."

Rhiann attempted to argue, but Lon shaking his head changed her mind. She let it go.

The first rays of dawn broke through the sky as the posse took charge of the outlaws. Satisfied that all was under control, the sheriff gave his order. "All right, let's mount these hardcases up and get 'em moving. We got a long day ahead of us."

For the next half hour during which breaking daylight dimly lit the scene, horses were saddled and outlaws forced onto them, their hands secured. The posse mounted and surrounded their charges, ready for the long ride back to Ironsight. Electing to overload the camp's buckboard and to double up on the few remaining horses, the liberated prisoners set out on their own journey back to Colinas de Oro. The sheriff approached Lon and Rhiann, now seated on the steps of the cook shack.

"Pearce, it was… interesting working with you. Not what I'd call a pleasure, but I got to tell you, you do get things done, you and your wife both. Thanks for your help."

Lon looked up, not giving an inch. "Didn't do it for you."

"I know, but thanks anyway. You made my job a good deal easier. I'm glad you two got back together. It looks like you could use a revolver. I see your holster is empty. The men found this one. Want it?"

"Yup."

Martín handed over the weapon, then voiced another thought. "Something else to think about. I'm going to need a deputy in Colinas de Oro. Job's yours if you want it." He held the badge out.

Lon shook his head. "Sheriff, reckon I'd tell you what you can do with that badge, but they's a lady present. Far as that town's concerned, I'd be right content not ever setting foot there again. Once was enough. We'll be moving on up north."

"Can't say I blame you there. Look, some of the men from the town tell me Garand had gold stashed around here. Once thing's calm down, they'll probably come back to get it. I'd say it's their due. If you can find it first, you're welcome to whatever you can carry. I'd consider it payment for your time here and look the other way."

"Reckon we'll take you up on that. We'll need some startup money, we get to Oregon."

Martín cocked his head. "Guess I'll get going. Got to find that woman and track down a crazy man. This ought to be fun. Better get to it." He touched a hand to his hat and walked to his horse. Taking the lead, he set the posse and their prisoners on the road out of the canyon.

Lon got up. "Let's find that gold and get shed of this place."

Rhiann smiled. "I know exactly where it is. I saw him bury it. I'll show you. First—she pointed at the cabin—"Garand kept all the guns in there. I'm going to find mine."

Seconds later, she emerged with her Colt Lightning in hand. She dropped it into her holster. "That's better. Now, the gold." She led him behind the cabin to the spot where Hirsch's body had been buried. About six feet away, closer to the north slope, a neatly packed mound of earth was her objective. "Right there."

Lon went to the cabin's back wall where a shovel had been propped. The increasing daylight afforded easy access to the soft ground. The shovel made short work of it. In a few minutes, he unearthed several canvas sacks, tied at their tops with rawhide thongs. He opened one, peering inside.

"Whooee! They's got to be a fortune here." He counted the sacks still in the hole. "Better'n a dozen pokes."

Rhiann was hesitant, glancing around. "I've got a funny feeling about this. Can we just take what we can carry and get away from this place?"

Lon nodded. "Good idea." He tied off the thong on the open sack and reached to pick up another. Rhiann secured two as well, and they started around the cabin to where Gray stood. They deposited two sacks in each of the pouches. Lon looked to the corral. "I'll saddle your horse. We can fill your saddlebags, as well."

"I'll get a couple more." Rhiann walked back to the stash while Lon headed for the corral.

When he returned, leading Rhiann's freshly saddled horse, Rhiann had already fetched two more similarly secured pouches, and stood waiting in front of the cabin. They set to work loading her saddlebags, paying little heed to anything but the job at hand. A sound behind them took Lon's attention too late.

"Don't move. Don't even twitch."

They froze as they both recognized the voice. Lon did some quick ciphering. After Garand got missed in the fracas, he likely crawled off into the shaft and spent the night in there, hiding in plain sight.

"Turn around slowly." Garand's voice was a snarl. "Keep your hands where I can see 'em."

Lon nodded to Rhiann. They turned to face Garand, their hands at shoulder level. Garand stood with his revolver trained on them. At this range, he couldn't miss and Lon couldn't risk outdrawing a bullet. His mind began working on a plan. It depended on Rhiann successfully distracting Garand, allowing Lon time to act. Glancing at her, he hoped she'd figure it out. She nodded, almost imperceptibly.

"Now, one at a time, with your left hands only, lift out your guns and toss them away." Garand's gaze fell to Rhiann. "You first."

Rhiann reached out her revolver and heaved it off to her right.

"Now you."

Lon followed the order, pitching his new weapon to his left.

"Good. I watched you from the shaft, loading up my gold, but that's as far as you'll get. You've taken the mine from me, but you'll not take my gold. I worked too hard to allow that." He looked directly at Lon. "Take those sacks from your saddlebags and place them on the ground. If you do anything but that, anything at all, I'll kill your woman." He made a show of moving his aim to Rhiann.

Lon considered trying to keep the man talking as a distraction to play for time to concoct a way out of this, but he discarded the thought. Nothing could outrun the bullet meant for Rhiann. No, he'd have to comply and depend on Rhiann's intelligence to give him the chance he needed. Moving slowly, he turned to Gray and opened the saddlebag.

Rhiann's voice broke the silence. "Why should we cooperate?"

Lon, his back to Garand, cracked a smile. She'd got the message. "What?"

Rhiann had Garand's full attention. "You're going to kill us anyway. Why should we make it easier for you?"

Garand hesitated as Lon's hand, inside the saddlebag, touched metal. "Shut up!"

Lon gripped the butt of the Colt hard. His thumb eased the hammer back, recalling Garand had not cocked his weapon, providing more time.

Rhiann continued the distraction. "You're such a big man, why don't you shut me up?"

Now or never. In one smooth motion, Lon pulled the Colt out, spun, and dropped to a knee as the hammer fell on the capped nipple. The gun barked, spewing white smoke. The round hit its mark in Garand's chest, knocking him backward. Lon fired again, hitting the man higher in the diaphragm. He staggered back farther, futilely trying to cock his weapon. Lon's third shot dropped Garand on his back, spread-eagle.

Advancing cautiously, Lon held his aim on the man. He kicked the revolver from Garand's hand and took a knee to check for life signs. Glancing back at Rhiann, he shook his head. Dead. Rhiann breathed a noticeable sigh of relief.

Lon got up and went to Rhiann. She let herself fall into his waiting one-arm embrace as his gun hand rested the Colt along his leg, pointed at the ground. They remained there for what seemed like an hour instead of the moments it actually took. Rhiann collected herself. Lon held her close.

"Thank God for that gun." There was a nervous twitch to her voice.

Lon smiled. "God and Toby Joe Hawks."

"Yeah, him too. I'd say we make a pretty good team, you and I."

Lon nodded. "Mighty well told. What do you say we finish up and get the hell out of here?"

"Works for me."

Lon spent a few minutes collecting their guns, then assembling supplies to load on their pack mule, still in the corral. When the mule was packed and ready, they mounted. Lon took a final look around.

"Lon, wait."

He turned to see a pensive, worried Rhiann a few feet behind him.

"We can't leave her."

"Come again?"

"Mildred. We can't let the sheriff find her. He'll take her back to her husband, back to the same situation. We have to find her first, help her get away from that."

Lon turned Gray to face her. "We'd be horning in where we don't belong."

"Maybe so, but she needs help, Lon, real help. Help only we can give her. We have to."

Lon was silent as he thought about it. She was right. The sheriff would follow the law and return Mildred to her legal next of kin, that being her husband. To hear Rhiann tell it, that sidewinder'd end up beating the hell out of her, or worse, just for fun. Couldn't let that happen. He swung down from the saddle.

"Lon?"

"Reckon I'll put the mule up again, saddle a mount for her, 'less'n you reckon she can walk to wherever she's going."

Rhiann flashed a warm grin at him.

20

THE RIDE TO THE POSSE campsite went quickly. Not much remained of the abandoned cold camp save for some torn up ground and the figure of a woman frantically searching the area. Lon and Rhiann increased speed, catching up with Grace in her wandering. They pulled up nearby. As they dismounted, she looked around.

"Rhiann." She hurried to them, in a somewhat anxious state. "Thank God you've come. I'm worried sick. Mildred's run off."

Rhiann went to Grace and put a comforting hand on her arm. "That's why we're here. Did the sheriff leave you out here alone?"

Grace nodded. "I convinced them I could help take care of Mildred when they found her. While they're out looking for her, I've been trying to find her tracks, but I have no idea what I'm doing."

Lon joined them. "I know a mite about tracking. Whereabouts was she when she run off?"

"I'll show you." Grace led them to a spot away from the section the main body of men had occupied and from where the horses had been hobbled. Less surface disturbance existed here. She pointed. "There."

Lon stopped the two women. "Stay here. Let me have a look-see." He moved forward in a wide circle, concentrating on the ground. Slowly he closed on the spot Grace had pointed out, narrowing his arc. Several times he stopped to crouch for closer examination. Re-moving a glove, he ran his hand carefully over spots of interest, then moved on, finally reaching the area the deputy and the two women had occupied. "Bedrolls here." That was almost inaudible. He went to a knee and scrutinized the ground where they had lain, finally decid-ing which had been Mildred's.

Rhiann and Grace watched with interest as Lon seemed to iden-tify Mildred's footprints. "Smallest tracks here. Heap of pacing." He moved slightly farther out, staying close to the ground, feeling for tracks. "That way." He pointed out with his hand the direction she had taken. "She's heading west." He rose.

Grace looked in the direction. "There's nothing out there. Where is she going?"

"Don't reckon she knows. Just… looking to get away."

"Will you be able to find her?"

"I can track her, but it'll be slow. Got to walk it. Can't promise nothing. Stay back a me a-ways. Bring the horses on with you." He headed out, stooped over, scouring the earth in front of him, moving slow. The women, leading the horses, followed at a safe distance to prevent obscuring the trail ahead.

After about ten minutes, they'd covered little ground. The rem-nants of the campsite were still visible behind them. Lon stopped, passing an ungloved hand over the earth. "Shifted again." He aimed his hand generally southwest, then continued following the tracks.

Moments later, he observed another change. The footprints now went northwest. Then he stopped. "Pears she fell here, crawled a mite." He glanced in the direction the tracks seemed to take. "On her feet again here. Stumbling, dragging her feet." Sighting the obstacle ahead, a mild slope leading to a rise a short distance away, he moved in a hurry toward the ridge. The women followed, closer now.

Lon halted at the crest of the rise. The women closed on him as he gazed down the opposite slope, pointing to a figure at the base, a woman. Rhiann and Grace joined him. "Got her." He started down the grade, going quickly.

It took him only a few seconds to reach the figure, face down, her dress soiled and in shreds. He crouched and rolled her carefully on her back. She was close to unconscious. Her hands and face were grimy and bore scrapes and cuts.

Rhiann and Grace reached them quickly. Grace sucked in a frightened breath. "Oh, God." Rhiann instinctively grabbed the canteen from Gray's saddle and went to Mildred. She pulled the cork and handed it to Lon as he put an arm behind the woman's head to lift her slightly.

"Reckon she fell again up top, rolled down to here. Pretty banged up." He applied the tip of the canteen to Mildred's lips and let a few drops pass over her mouth. She stirred. Her eyelids fluttered. He allowed a few more drops to fall. Her mouth opened. He stopped the flow. "Mildred, come on now. Come back to me." She seemed to respond to the sound of his voice. Her eyes opened to small slits, eyelids blinking quickly, intermittently. "That's it. Come on back."

She roused, then came abruptly awake, instantly alarmed. Involuntary movements forced her body to try shrinking away from an unknown perceived threat.

"Whoa now." Lon spoke quietly, calmly. "Easy. Nobody's going to hurt you. You're safe now." He hesitated, letting his words sink in.

Slowly, she settled down. Lon offered water, sparingly. That brought her around a bit more.

After several minutes, Mildred became more lucid, attempting to sit up. Lon helped her. "Where... where am I? I don't... I don't know what happened."

"Near as I can tell, you took a tumble down that grade back there." He pointed with his chin. "Might could a been out of it when you fell. You got some nasty cuts there."

She raised her hands to explore the wounds.

"You just sit there till you feel better. Here, take some more water."

Another few minutes passed before Mildred felt up to talking. "I had to get away. I can't go back there. I won't." A tear peeked out from the corner of her eye and ran down her cheek.

Lon leaned in closer to whisper to her. "Ain't nobody making you do that."

Rhiann and Grace crowded around her.

Rhiann spoke quietly. "You don't have to worry about that. We'll help you."

Somewhat frantically, Mildred tried to make her point. "I have to get away from him. He'll beat me again, I know he will."

Grace shook her head. "No he won't. Never again."

Mildred sank into sobs, then broke down.

Lon looked up. "Reckon maybe it's better you… see to her."

Rhiann crouched and put her arm around Mildred's shoulders. Lon got up. Grace moved in on Mildred's other side. Both women consoled her.

Looking on from a standing position, Lon was certain he'd made the right call to step back. Rhiann and Grace did a better job of comforting her.

Gray's whinny drew their attention. Someone coming. Lon glanced around to see two horsemen crest the ridge above. His hand instinctively went to his holster as he strained to identify the strangers. As they descended, he made out one familiar figure and backed off, his hand poised over his gun. "Sheriff's coming."

"No, please." Mildred shrank back. "Don't let him take me back."

"That ain't happening." Lon's voice was low, resolute.

Sheriff Martín and Des, the posse member who'd been assigned to guard the women, drew rein at the base of the grade.

Lon stood between them and the women. "Sheriff." It was a tentative greeting.

Martín looked surprised. "Pearce. Thought I'd seen the last of you."

"Yeah, well, you know, bad penny and all."

The sheriff leaned forward, placing his hands on the saddle horn. "I see you've done our job for us again, found the woman."

"Yup."

"Well, thanks for that. We'll take it from here, see her back where she belongs."

"See, now, that's… going to be a problem."

Martín was puzzled. "How's that?"

"She don't want to go back there. Wants to go a different way."

The sheriff took a breath, showing a determined look. "Pearce, I'll tell you what I told your wife. The law says she's got to go back to her husband. That's—"

"Law's wrong. You know that, well as I do. You want her, you got to go through me."

Rhiann came to her feet. "And me."

Grace backed them up, still crouched and holding Mildred's shoulders. "And me."

Martín's expression changed to annoyance as his intense stare focused on Lon. "You know where this is going, don't you?"

"Reckon so." Lon steeled himself.

"I'm going to ask you one time, step aside."

Lon shook his head, his tongue wetting his lower lip. "Sorry, Sheriff, I ain't moving." He stood his ground, resolved, gun hand poised.

Rhiann took a step forward. "Sheriff, are you married?"

"Ma'am?"

"I asked if you're married."

He shot her a sidewise glance. "I am, but I don't see—"

"Do you beat your wife?"

Martín frowned. "Course not. What kind a—"

"Well, Mildred's husband does. He smacks her around just for the enjoyment of it. Is that the kind of life you want to send her back to? So he can maybe maim or kill her next time? Do you want to be responsible for that? How will you explain that to your wife? Can you live with that on your conscience?"

The sheriff came up short, taking a long pause.

Rhiann pressed it home. "Well, can you?"

Martín shifted uncomfortably in his saddle. "Well… when you put it that way, I guess not."

"Then help us stop that once and for all. We can put Mildred on a train going anywhere she chooses so she can start a new life away from that god-awful man."

Martín huffed, then, after a long, thoughtful silence, he turned to his companion. "Des, you listen hard. You and me, we were never here. Never came across these folks, never found the woman. Nothing more's to be said or done about this. She's in the wind. Savvy?"

Des nodded, the hint of a smile on his face.

The sheriff pulled his horse around and headed up the slope. Des tipped his hat, now sporting a broad grin. He followed his boss.

Without taking his eyes off the retreating lawmen, Lon relaxed his hand. "Got to hand it to you. You surely know how to head off a showdown."

Rhiann's concerned expression continued. "Couldn't have you drawing down on the law. Amnesty, remember?"

"I remember. You learned me good on that one. But I'd a never took it far as you thought I might would. Ciphered on him rolling over 'fore it came to that. He cottons to playing it safe-like."

"Well, you could've fooled me."

"Uh-huh. Fooled him too."

CAREFULLY, GENTLY, RHIANN AND GRACE saw to Mildred's wounds and cleaned her up as much as was possible in the wilderness. After some time to regain her composure, they helped her onto the spare horse, and with Grace riding double behind Rhiann, the party set out for the mine.

Lon halted them at the beginning of the entrance road. "Wait here a spell. They's things needs doing." He rode on into the camp alone, fetched a blanket from the cabin, and covered Garand's body. Then he signaled the women to proceed.

They entered the camp as Lon stood near Gray, waiting. He helped Mildred and Grace down from the horses. Rhiann dismounted and joined him. He whispered a request to her to give him a hand behind the cabin. She nodded.

The women stood idly, curiosity obvious in their expressions.

"We'll be right back." Lon led Rhiann to the pit behind the cabin where the gold had been buried. He stopped, turned, and took her in his arms. Their eyes met. She seemed to know what was on his mind as he leaned in. He met her lips with his as she melted into the kiss, one long overdue. When he leaned back seconds later, a tear was evident at the corner of his eye. "God, I was afraid I'd lose you."

She held tight to his frame. Her voice cracked a bit with emotion. "You'll never lose me."

Their embrace joined them as one as they each held on to the love for the other that would never die. He sniffled back the tears threatening to break free and cleared his throat. That generated a chuckle from Rhiann that signaled the end of the moment. He leaned back, whispering to her. "Later."

She grinned. "Always."

He pulled in a cleansing breath and turned his attention to the pit. Squatting down, he lifted two sacks of the gold nuggets still remaining there. As he rose, she reached for one of the sacks, appearing to know his intention.

"I'll take one."

Smiling, they walked around to rejoin Mildred and Grace, still waiting near the horses. Lon brought his pouch to Grace. "Don't reckon Garand'll miss this now. Should ought to help you do what you want to do."

Grace took it, smiling. "Thank you."

Rhiann moved closer to Mildred but kept her attention on Grace. "What will you do now?"

"I'm going back to Colinas de Oro. Those people need my help and so does Rita. I'm not going to let her slip back into her old ways. We've made too much progress. I guess if anything good came from this experience, it has to be Rita's change of heart and Mildred's second chance at living. I'll go on from there."

Lon shook his head. "I admire what you're trying to do, but, truth be told, I wouldn't give you a plugged nickel for your chances at saving that town. They should a been out beating the bushes for them missing folks 'stead a staying snug at home. But I reckon with your grit, you might could get 'em closer'n they deserve."

Grace's smile broadened. "I hope so." She hefted the sack. "I really appreciate this." She looked around at the camp, then back to the others. "I'll be going now. I'll put this to good use." She hugged each one of them, secured the gold sack, and mounted the spare horse. "God bless you all. I pray He smiles on you." She turned the horse up the road. They watched as she slowly rode away.

"Reckon it's about time we get to getting as well." Lon strode to the corral to saddle the last remaining horse. He led the mount, along with the mule already trail outfitted, to where the women stood.

Rhiann handed the bag of gold she'd been holding to Mildred. "You'll need this to find your way to a new home. We'll stay with you until you can get on a train."

Mildred accepted it with an embarrassed smile, placing it carefully in her saddlebag. "Thank you. But I've caused you so much trouble already. I shouldn't take you out of your way. I'm sure I can do this on my own."

Lon looked her in the eye. "No disrespect, ma'am. When we come on you, you was headed every way but the right one. Ain't taking a chance on you getting turned around again. We'll side you."

"But—"

Rhiann flashed a smile. "No buts. Oregon's waited this long. A little longer won't matter."

Lon went to Gray and mounted. Gray pranced around a bit, obviously ready to go. "Plenty a daylight left. Time we put this godforsaken place in the yonder. Head out."

DESPITE BEING A BORN-AND-bred New Yorker who lived most of his life in New Jersey, Bob Giel was a cowboy at heart and lived by the cowboy code. When most of the world today laughs at the quaint and seemingly antiquated concept of honor, he embodied it. Always faithful. Always loyal. Always giving his best effort. Always honest. And perhaps most importantly, keeping his word no matter what. Those values weren't just an act or an affectation, but something he worked at and recommitted to every day. Sadly, Bob passed away in early 2023, but his work and his ethos will continue to live on in his writing.